Never-Ending Promises

by

Angela Lam

Never-Ending Promises

Cover Art by *Diana Carlile*

The Wild Rose Press, Inc.
PO Box 708
Adams Basin, NY 14410-0708
Visit us at www.thewildrosepress.com

Publishing History
First Edition, 2023
Trade Paperback ISBN 978-1-5092-4670-0
Digital ISBN 978-1-5092-4671-7

Published in the United States of America

Scowling, Deb leaned forward. "Are you saying he doesn't love me because he's battling cancer?"

"Possibly." Dr. Chang met her gaze for a moment before glancing at Cassidy. "Before your diagnosis, how did you feel about Deb?"

Cassidy shrugged. "I don't know. We just went about our routine. Everything was fine. I didn't have to think or feel anything."

Dr. Chang raised his eyebrows and uncurled his fingers one at a time. "You avoided your relationship through work, alcohol, sports, Adam, and poetry."

"Poetry?" Deb snickered. "He hasn't written since he self-published his book of poems two Christmases ago."

"Maybe poetry is the solution and not the problem." Dr. Chang steepled his fingers. "Have you been journaling any poetry?"

"Not poetry. Just thoughts and feelings as they surface."

Cassidy stared at his hands. For the first time since high school, the nail beds were clean and the pads of his fingers were smooth. He stretched his fingers, aching for the woodsy smell of lumber, the buzz of saws, the whack of nails, and the satisfaction of watching a building rise up from the dirt. Writing was a lot like construction, laying one word after another, erecting a story from the ground of his thoughts. "I don't write poems. I just jot down whatever comes to mind— nothing formal." The words, once bright and hopeful with lyricism, twisted into darkness and despair. Why share those thoughts with anyone?

Praise for Angela Lam

"NOW AND FOREVER: A richly emotional tale of what it takes to keep later-in-life romance on track. With equal parts honesty, heart, and depth, Angela Lam weaves a story to remind us that love is all we really ever need."

~Karen Booth, author

~*~

"NOW AND FOREVER provides a realistic, thoughtful portrayal of a mature marriage at a crossroads."

~Liz Crowe, Amazon Best-Selling, Award-Winning Author of WHAT HAPPENS IN DENVER

~*~

"The author has skillfully crafted an utterly addictive and explosive story of trust, second love, and fortitude, mixed with a splash of an indelible commitment between an indigenous American widow and a billionaire with a heart. You won't be able to put it down until you've learned to LOVE AGAIN."

~Jerry Aylward, author

~*~

"Anyone who understands the difficulties of weight loss, the sweetness of sharing the struggle and the power of friendship will want to gobble up Angela Lam's heartfelt FRIENDS FIRST."

~Mary K. Tilgham, author

Dedication

For Ed and Lina

"All time is now."
Hope "Spirit Walk" Spencer Gold,
Wapi Medicine Woman

Chapter One

Cassidy Burke sat in Dr. Prasad's office, which faced the glistening, glass-and-steel structure of Vine Valley Bank, the tallest building located in Northern California, outside of San Francisco. A swell of pride puffed his chest, remembering how he and his father fastened each nine-foot-tall window weighing over one hundred fifty pounds. He couldn't believe the building was twenty-five years old. His son, Adam, was only five at the time, and he was married to his first wife, Stephanie.

So much had changed, including his health. What started as a tickle at the back of his throat at the beginning of softball season evolved into difficulty swallowing by the Fourth of July. Lately, he tired from carrying an armload of lumber or running the bases during a softball tournament. Something was definitely wrong, but how wrong he didn't know. He perched at the edge of the vinyl chair, jiggling his legs.

"The results of the biopsy and positron emission tomography scan are back." Dr. Prasad folded his hands on the desk and gazed directly into Cassidy's eyes. "You have throat cancer."

Cassidy stopped his jittery legs. The cold air of the room rushed around him. Goose bumps erupted on his hairy forearms, and sweat beaded across his forehead. *Cancer*. A whirlwind of emotions swarmed through his chest and down his arms. A flurry of thoughts fumbled. *How will I handle my business? How will I finish the softball season with the Vine Valley Crushers?* He gulped. *How will I survive?* With the back of his hand, he wiped the perspiration from his forehead and grimaced. "How did I get this disease?"

Dr. Prasad shrugged. "It's common in people fifty-five and older. Smoking and drinking increase the risks. But certain viruses can be culprits." He picked up the phone and dialed an extension. "You may come in and meet the patient." He set the handset in the cradle and gathered a few papers on the desk. "I'm transferring your file to Dr. Rodriguez, who will oversee your care."

Cassidy froze, but his thoughts spiraled out of control. This kind, old family doctor diagnosed Adam's cerebral palsy and autism. He stopped by the ICU every day while Cassidy's parents lay dying. Why couldn't he manage Cassidy's cancer?

Three raps knocked on the door.

Jumping, Cassidy couldn't keep his thoughts from tumbling out of his mouth. "What are my chances of living?"

"Good, if the treatment is successful." Dr. Prasad stood, and his white lab coat fluttered open, exposing a blue button-down shirt and navy slacks. He wagged his finger. "But you never can be sure in these situations." He dashed across the room and opened the door.

A small woman in her thirties strode across the industrial gray carpet and extended a hand. "I'm Dr. Rodriguez, your oncologist."

Frowning, Cassidy swept his gaze along the length of her body. She was pretty with long, black hair fastened into a low ponytail and a black dress peeking beneath the hem of her white lab coat. He stood on wobbly knees and shook her hand. "Cassidy Burke, your patient." She had dark, serious eyes and full, pouty lips. He imagined she was used to telling people bad news and crying with them.

"Pleased to meet you." After flashing a smile, she grasped the file from Dr. Prasad and gestured toward the door. "My office is down the hall."

Her brusque, professional demeanor unsettled him. He followed her into a tiny, windowless room smelling of chamomile tea. A standard desk and three chairs filled the small space. The room felt sterile and impersonal. He shivered, wishing he could return to the familiar comfort of Dr. Prasad's more intimate office.

She set the file on the desk and motioned toward the chairs.

After sinking into a plush seat, Cassidy folded his hands in his lap.

With a no-nonsense demeanor, she slipped a pair of reading glasses over the bridge of her nose and scanned his medical records. Nodding, she closed the folder and wiggled the mouse to refresh the computer screen. "For the best results, I'm recommending an aggressive treatment of chemotherapy to stop the spread of the cancer followed by radiation to eliminate the tumor. Starting Monday, you'll come into the clinic every day for twelve weeks. Then you'll have another PET scan before Thanksgiving to evaluate the progress."

How cruel and heartless those harsh words sounded. Each syllable crumbled against his understanding like bricks blasted from a condemned building.

After a few keystrokes, she grabbed a sheet of

paper from the printer. "Here's your schedule."

Gaping, he eyed the list of dates, times, and locations until his vision blurred. How could he go on working or caring for Adam? He felt his already sore throat tighten as his personal world narrowed to treat this disease.

She tugged the keyboard closer and leaned back in her chair. "You'll want someone to drive you to and from your appointments, even on the days you feel well. Do you have someone reliable?" She gave him a sidelong glance.

"My wife." He folded the paper into fours and tucked it into his shirt pocket. Deb shouldn't mind tagging along. After all, when her mother was diagnosed with lung cancer five years ago, she endured this routine. "If she's taking care of my son, I have some friends I can call." He thought of Nick, who set his own hours, and Lionel, who wasn't working while his store was being rebuilt.

"Good." She flashed a smile and tapped on the computer keyboard. "You have any other commitments coming up?"

Her voice lifted at the end of the question. He rubbed his jaw, the stubble abrasive against his fingertips. "My softball team plays out-of-town tournaments twice a month." He tensed. "Are you suggesting I quit the rest of the season?" A prickle of fear rippled across his scalp. Pitching always centered him, and right now, he needed that stability.

Nodding, she continued typing. "You don't know how your body will respond to treatment. The dose of radiation is low, so you won't lose your hair. A lot of patients are too weak to work, and some experience side effects requiring hospitalization." She twisted her lips into a frown. "You might also need a feeding tube since your mouth will be full of sores. Swallowing will be more painful." She stopped typing and swiveled in her chair to face him. "Radiation basically burns through to the cellular level. You might even lose your voice."

He touched his throat and swallowed. The saliva was a slim blade slicing from tongue to stomach. How much worse could the pain get?

"You'll want to find something relaxing to focus your mind. A lot of people learn meditation." She waved a hand. "Avoid depressing things like watching the news."

"Anything else?" Gripping the arms of the chair, he steadied his body against the unrelenting torrent of bad news. He didn't want to ask, but he needed to know.

"Don't worry. A lot of people survive."

He exhaled a breath of relief and released his sweaty hands from the arms of the chair. When he glimpsed the sadness in her eyes, he felt the peace disappear. Obviously, she knew some patients who died. He wanted to ask what percentage of her patients lived, but he knew better. Privacy laws would prevent an honest answer. He watched her lips moving, but he no longer heard the words she spoke. The panic rising at the back of his throat made him long for a beer—something cold and bitter to numb all of his nerve endings. *Twelve weeks*. He didn't want to consider how this diagnosis would change his life. He was the best pitcher for the Vine Valley Crushers, the sole owner of the construction company his father left him, and the primary caregiver for his thirty-year-old disabled son.

All of his adult life he had taken care of others. How could he learn to take care of himself?

****

A rush of warm air swept through the house before the front door slammed shut. Deb startled, dropping the altar linen on the living room carpet. "Cassidy?" Kneeling, she plucked the fallen fabric from the floor and tossed it onto the couch before rushing into the hallway.

Cassidy's heavy footfalls stomped through the foyer and into the kitchen. He hunched his broad shoulders to his ears and tugged his Vine Valley Crushers baseball cap over his forehead.

She halted. *The news must be bad.* Her heartbeat hammered in her chest, and her breathing stuttered. *What did Dr. Prasad say?*

Behind her, Adam pattered down the hallway. He was a grown man, but he wobbled like a toddler. He thrust a computer tablet into her hands. "Song!"

She swiped a trembling finger across the screen and scrolled through the playlist to find Nirvana's "Never Mind."

Before the drumbeat started, he yanked the computer tablet out of her hands, scampered down the hallway to his room, and shut the door.

With a deep breath, she treaded across the linoleum floor in the kitchen. "What did Dr. Prasad say?"

Cassidy slumped at the kitchen table. He took a swig of beer and glanced down and away. "Fine."

She pieced together the telltale signs of his lie, from his rigid jaw to the half-drunk bottle of beer. Standing beside him, she plunged a hand into a pants pocket and rubbed her trembling fingers across smooth, cool rosary beads. *Jesus, Mary, Joseph, pray for us.* The lifelong habit could not unravel the tightness braiding up the backs of her legs. "Please, tell me the truth."

After gulping down the last swallow, he shuddered and winced. He banged the empty bottle onto the table. "I have throat cancer."

Not again. She hitched her breath. Five years ago, she lost her mother to lung cancer. The memories surfaced like buoys on the ocean of her mind, her fears dogpaddling between them. *Don't take him away, God.* Tears pricked the edges of her lashes, and her throat closed. *Take me. I'm the one who deserves to be punished. I'm the one who broke my vows and left the convent. Not him.* The clatter of a chair hitting the floor jostled her ashore.

Cassidy set the chair upright, kicking it against the edge of the round table, before striding across the room and opening the fridge. With one deft motion, he grabbed another beer and popped off the lid. Foam spurted to the top, and he shoved the geyser into his mouth. With each gulp, he closed his eyes and flinched.

She strode over to wrestle the bottle from his hand. "If you have cancer, you shouldn't be drinking."

Tightening his grip on the bottle, he waved her aside.

She stumbled back a couple of steps, and her hips bumped against the kitchen sink. Oh, why couldn't he learn to control his temper? Between him and Adam, she was always jostled around like a table tennis ball. Neither one of them intended to throw her off balance, but the behavior annoyed her.

Adam bustled into the kitchen, carrying the

computer tablet, which played a guitar riff. As soon as his gaze landed on Cassidy, he widened his eyes. "Dad." He shoved the computer tablet against Cassidy's chest. "Song."

Deb stood by the sink, watching the curious and familiar dance between father and son.

With studied grace, Cassidy grasped the computer tablet with one hand, the beer bottle in the other. "Use your finger." He showed the screen to Adam.

Adam scrolled through the list of songs with the tip of his index finger and tapped his selection. Soft sounds of a piano floated into the room.

"Good job, buddy." Cassidy grinned, releasing the computer tablet and taking a swallow of beer.

A pang of jealousy squeezed Deb's chest. Why couldn't she help Adam the way Cassidy did? She heaved a sigh. Maybe if she had been with the young man from the moment of his birth, tailoring her life around the boy's existence, then she would know what to do. Her inclusion into their lives produced an unexpected wedge. She wondered if Cassidy's ex-wife, Stephanie, was a better mom. Guilt seized her breath. *Why did I rip apart this family?*

Adam held the speaker against an ear and smiled.

He looked like a younger version of his father. They shared the same sandy curls tousled over the ears and a spate of freckles across the nose. They were almost the same height, with Adam an inch shorter. Cassidy was broader, with sloped shoulders from carrying lumber up ladders and a pot belly from drinking too much beer. Adam was long and lanky with the awkward gestures of a young man who didn't know how to control his arms and legs.

Smiling, Cassidy patted Adam's shoulder.

Deb stepped away from the kitchen sink.

Adam rushed out of the room.

Crossing her arms over her chest, Deb balanced her weight between her feet. "What will the doctor do?"

Cassidy shrugged. "Chemo, radiation, the works." He patted his breast pocket. "I have the schedule here."

Nodding, Deb stepped closer. She didn't know anything about throat cancer, but she suspected alcohol didn't help. She held out a hand. "Give me the beer."

Cassidy glowered, inching backward. He swallowed the last drops and wiped foam from his mouth with the back of a hand.

She stood still, not daring to touch him. Why did he defy her like a child? Tension rose like heat between them. She plunged a hand into her pocket and clutched her rosary beads.

"Aren't you supposed to trust God will take care of everything?" Cassidy tossed the empty bottle in the recycling bin beneath the sink. He flung his cap onto the counter and threw open his arms. "I promise I won't die."

When he stood with his arms outstretched, he reminded her of Jesus hanging on the cross. Shaking her head, she shuddered. "We're being punished for breaking our vows. Me, to God. You, to Stephanie."

"Isn't God supposed to forgive?" He wrapped her in his arms.

Cassidy was right. When she confessed her sins years ago, God forgave her. Why did her atheist husband have more faith? She tucked her sharp chin against his firm, warm chest. He smelled sour with beer and salty with fear. Sobs wracked her body. After releasing the rosary in her pocket, she clawed his T-shirt. The soft material knotted in a fist. *What will I do without you?* She closed her eyes and prayed. *Please, God help us. Cure Cassidy of this disease. Help me to learn how to be a better stepmother.* She shuddered. *And, most importantly, please, help me forgive myself like you've already forgiven me.*

Chapter Two

The next day, Cassidy drove his pickup truck along the back roads leading to the construction site of Larry's Deli. The summer sun broke through the fog, and the vineyards lining the country roads peaked like golden hands praying to heaven. He didn't believe in God like Deb did, but he trusted the breathtaking beauty of nature. Sunlight climbed the rolling hills and tumbled down to the Wapi River winding through Vine Valley to the Pacific Ocean. He and his parents settled here before he started high school. Over the years, the changes to the town left him yearning for simpler days when Wapi Mountain belonged to the tribe and the casino didn't engulf the flatlands. If the winery business didn't dominate the area, these few patches of open fields and meadows would be swallowed by new construction. Business would be great, but the tranquility surrounding the mountain and the river would be gone.

The closer he drove to downtown, buildings and streetlights sprouted like weeds. Soon he entered the grid-like maze of suburban streets leading to what would once again be Larry's Deli. He steered into the parking lot and tucked the truck beneath the shade of a surviving oak tree from the fire that burned down this neighborhood treasure almost two years ago. The rumors were almost as bad as the truth—a domestic dispute between an employee and her boyfriend caused the flames. Luckily, no one was hurt. Only the building was destroyed.

He hopped out of the truck, placed his hands on his hips, and squinted at the progress. The afternoon heat shimmered in waves and blistered through his T-shirt.

With the concrete foundation poured and the steel framing erected, his crew was busy putting in the siding and leaving room for the windows and sliding glass doors.

A few moments later, Lionel's delivery truck lumbered into the parking lot. Lionel climbed out of the cab and shut the door. "Hey, Romeo, are we still on track for our grand re-opening?"

He was a short, stout man with long, white hair and a gait creaky from arthritis.

A smirk played at the corners of Cassidy's lips. That old nickname from high school still warmed his heart—poetry was the way to a woman's soul. The smile faded. When was the last time he wrote a poem? Never mind. He shifted the focus back to business and clapped a hand on his friend's shoulder. "We're right on target." The store was scheduled to open at the end of October, which was twelve weeks away—the same time his cancer treatment ended. A knot tightened in his stomach. Would he be well enough to oversee the project so it finished on time?

For a long moment, he hesitated. He didn't know whether or not to confide his health crisis to Lionel. Not only was his friend the captain of the Vine Valley Crushers, but he was married to the town's biggest gossip. Cassidy wanted to continue playing softball, and he didn't want everyone to feel sorry for him and his family. He liked his privacy, which was one of the sticking points in his marriage to Stephanie. She was an actress seeking fame and fortune. He was a small-time contractor who only wanted to play ball. He had been approached by the major leagues while he was finishing college, but then Adam was born. Everything changed. He loosened his grip and tightened his lips. Once again, his whole life had tumbled upside down.

Lionel squinted from beneath the brim of his Vine Valley Crusher's baseball cap. "Something bothering you?"

Grumbling, Cassidy shoved his hands into his pockets. "If I tell you, then you need to keep it a secret."

Tossing back his head, Lionel laughed. "I learned from therapy never to keep a secret from my wife."

"Fine." Cassidy removed his hands from his pockets and folded both arms across his chest. He knew the reason for Lionel's reticence. Two years ago, a store employee, Michelle, asked Lionel to keep her unplanned pregnancy by her abusive boyfriend a secret. When Lionel refused to tell Geraldine, his high school sweetheart and wife of thirty-plus years, his marriage collapsed. Cassidy didn't know how the two repaired the damage through couples' therapy, but he did know they planned to renew their vows. "I'll keep the news to myself."

"Suit yourself." Lionel scratched the back of his neck. "I can't wait for this store to open. My kitchen and dining room have become a makeshift deli with Geraldine filling orders for sandwiches every single day of the week. The house constantly smells of pastrami on rye. Two extra refrigerators take up valuable real estate in my garage. I hate parking the truck in the driveway." He chuckled. "I want my home back."

"I hear you." Cassidy couldn't imagine storing his tools and heavy equipment at his tiny, ranch-style home. "I wish I could have sped up the process."

Lionel waved a hand. "Not your fault the city planners took twelve months to approve the plans."

The new blueprint for the store featured a state-of-the-art HVAC system, energy-efficient freezers, and a computerized point-of-sale system. Cassidy nodded. "As long as the supplies are delivered on time, my crew should finish on schedule."

A trilling sound erupted from Lionel's pocket. He grabbed the phone and swiped a finger across the screen. "Hello? Why, of course, I'd love to. See you soon." He smiled and shoved the phone into a pocket. "I'm leaving to babysit Michelle's baby. She has to work. See you at softball practice."

Cassidy grinned. "Have fun." After all the trouble Michelle caused—from the secret that nearly destroyed his marriage to the abusive boyfriend who burned down his store—she gave Lionel the one thing he had always wanted—a chance to nurture a child. Being a godfather was Lionel's greatest joy, much like Cassidy's pleasure in being a father to Adam.

After Lionel left, Cassidy grabbed his hard hat from the pickup truck and wandered closer to the building. He cupped his hands around his mouth. "Guillermo!" He waved to his foreman.

A nimble, young man in work boots hopped across the floor joists. "Yes, boss?"

Guillermo was a faithful employee. He always showed up on time and stayed until the day's work was finished. He never complained about working holidays or weekends. When a problem arose—with suppliers, the city inspectors, or the client—he always offered a reasonable solution. Out of all of his employees, Cassidy could trust this man to supervise the successful completion of Larry's Deli by the deadline. "I need to speak with you for a moment." He led the lanky man to the back of the lot bordering an orchard. "I'm promoting you to general manager and handing over operations to you."

"Why, boss?" Guillermo frowned, his dark mustache curling over his upper lip. "You have another project to manage?"

"No, I have—" He bit the inside of his mouth, hoping the pain would staunch the pressure building in the backs of his eyes. "Cancer. I start treatment soon, and I don't know how much longer I can work."

"Oh, no." Guillermo dropped his head and sighed. "Where? What stage?" He lifted his head and met his gaze.

"Throat." Cassidy shoved his hands into his pockets. "I didn't ask what stage. I don't want to know." Ignorance shielded him from contemplating worst-case scenarios. He needed to plan and not worry.

"No problem, boss. You can count on me. We'll get the job done." Guillermo clapped a hand on Cassidy's shoulder and squeezed.

The pressure of Guillermo's dark, broad hand reassured him. "Thanks, I'll increase your compensation and give you paid time off once the project is completed."

Guillermo shook his head. "No worries, boss. I have your back." He dropped his hand to his side.

"Remember Rosita? When she went into labor a month early, you gave me time off with pay. Before Junior started little league, you coached him. He's the best pitcher in his division because of you." He stepped back and waved toward the building under construction. "I know this project is extra special, because the building is for your friends. I won't let them down. You just focus on getting better. Okay?"

A splash of gratitude doused Cassidy, and he tugged his foreman into an awkward one-armed hug. "You're a good man, Guillermo. I'm lucky I can count on you."

"Don't worry, boss." Guillermo patted his back. "Rosita, Junior, and I will pray for you. With God, all things are possible."

Thinking of his wife, Cassidy nodded. Ever since he shared the news, he found her on her knees praying the rosary every day before he left for work. Frowning, he ground his heels into the dirt. For the first time in his life, he wished he believed in something bigger than himself.

****

Deb dipped her fingers into the cool holy water and made the sign of the cross, touching her forehead, her chest, and her left and right shoulders. After stepping into the dark mouth of the church's nave, she genuflected at the altar. She selected a pew and knelt on the red velvet cushion, lacing her hands together against the hard, wooden bench. Sunlight streamed through the stained glass windows. Jesus stretched his arms toward heaven, symbolizing the resurrection and ascension. The dank smells of must and candle wax lingered in the still air. Glancing around, she didn't see anyone she recognized. Not many people arrived this early to pray on a weekday. Most people were at work or enjoying the summer morning before the sweltering heat drove them inside to the sanctuary of air-conditioning.

Bowing her head, Deb closed her eyes and prayed. She prayed for Cassidy's full recovery, for Adam's cooperation, and for the stillness of her own heart. She also prayed for forgiveness.

The pew dipped and creaked with the weight of another parishioner.

The scent of cloves and citrus invaded her nostrils. With a quick, sidelong glance, she recognized Elliot. She braced her shoulders, tucked her head, and closed her eyes. *Go away.* Her jagged breath filled the narrow space between them. She hated Elliot for almost destroying Geraldine's marriage. What decent Catholic man seduced a married woman? Since the affair, Deb avoided patronizing Elliot's restaurant, Jasper's Bar and Grill. But she could not avoid him at the altar society where they both volunteered. Elliot's weakness for vulnerable women left a sour taste in Deb's mouth, and his nearness on the pew revived all sorts of bad memories she didn't want to deal with today. Why couldn't someone else have entered the church to pray—someone without a sordid history to remind her of her own mistakes and misgivings?

Elliot knelt close. "Morning, sober saint," he whispered.

His hot breath burned her ear. She shuddered, inching away. That old drinking and driving joke Geraldine told him would haunt Deb forever. She was sober, but she was not a saint. She committed adultery with a married man and broke up his family. So what if she married him and now cared for his disabled son? She was guilty just the same. "Glory be to the Father…" She prayed aloud, hoping to quiet Elliot.

When he clasped his hands, he jostled her shoulder and prayed along. "…and the Son, and the Holy Spirit."

Lifting her head, she swiveled her gaze. "I want to be alone with God."

"Then why be here in a public church?" He flashed a crooked smile.

She recognized the glint of mischief in his meadow-green eyes. "My husband has cancer, and I want to pray in God's home."

He crinkled his forehead. "I'm sorry."

The sincerity of his voice sliced through her. No wonder Geraldine had succumbed to his charms.

"I lost my wife five years ago to lymphoma." He blinked away the glassy sheen in his eyes. "I moved here to start over." He uncurled his clasped hands. "If you ever want to talk to someone, you know where to find me." Standing, he touched her shoulder. "Goodbye, my sober saint."

The warmth of his fingertips left impressions on her cotton shirt.

He slipped out of the pew and disappeared from the church.

Alone, Deb wondered if maybe he wasn't a scoundrel. Maybe he was a just a lonely man who lost his wife. He buried his grief in the pleasures of the body—just like she buried her guilt by constantly praying the rosary until the pads of her fingers grew calloused from rubbing the beads.

Chapter Three

After a long, tiring day at the construction site, Cassidy hopped into the stifling heat of the pickup truck and blasted the air-conditioning. As he drove home, he called Stephanie on his hands-free device. He wanted to speak with her before starting treatment, and he didn't want to call her from home. Between playing with Adam and helping Deb with dinner, he never had a moment of privacy.

The phone rang three times before she answered. "Hi, Cass. What's up?"

She sounded happy and carefree. He imagined her in costume—silver wig, skin-tight dress, and stacked heels. For the past two years, she starred as Mona, the matriarch of the Meddling family, on a popular streaming series called *Beyond Family*. Shortly after divorcing, she relocated to Los Angeles to pursue full-time acting. Since landing the plum role, she worked in Los Angeles ten months out of the year. When she wasn't filming, she lived in her brother's condo in Vine Valley and cared for Adam.

"Do you have time to talk?" He signaled right to take the back roads. Rows of trees lined the two-lane road. He smiled, remembering why he loved Vine Valley—the gentle blend of nature and suburban living in a tourist town complete with its own casino.

"Five, maybe ten minutes, before I have to shoot

another scene."

He steered onto another quiet street and drove along. Smiling, he remembered racing his used sports car on this narrow road. Where had the time gone? He swallowed and winced from the pain in his throat. "I have throat cancer."

"Cancer?"

Her voice rose to a shrill pitch.

"Unbelievable, right?" He steered over to a patch of dirt beneath a redwood tree just outside the Wapi Reservation, parked with the window rolled down, and turned off the engine. The heat saturated his cotton shirt. He tugged his cap over his forehead, shielding his eyes from the glare of the sun. "I don't smoke." He stopped, took a breath, and let the air settle at the bottom of his lungs.

"But you drink—a lot."

The sting of her words shot through him. He rubbed his eyes with his fists. He didn't drink *that* much—only a few beers after work or softball practice.

"I always begged you to stop."

Flinching, he recalled how she nagged him to cut back, switch to non-alcoholic beer, or attend a twelve-step program. But he didn't listen. He just drank some more.

"Have you quit now?"

He glanced away. A little booze never hurt anyone. "Cass?"

"I'm here." He sat upright, gazing at the still branches of the redwood trees. "I'm listening. I heard everything you said." He blinked.

"I'm sorry if I'm being harsh, but I'm thinking of Adam." She paused. "You're his whole world."

"I know." He rubbed a hand across his sweaty forehead. And Adam was the sun in his universe.

The line crackled with rustling sounds. "I have to go soon. How can I help?"

If I ask for her help, she'll lose everything she's worked for. How can I be that selfish? He tipped back his head, staring at the shadows playing against the redwood tree. "I need you to care for Adam over the next twelve weeks while I'm in treatment."

"What about Deb?"

The question knotted his shoulders. Deb babied Adam, selecting his playlist and spoon-feeding him meals when he was perfectly capable of both tasks given patience and time. "She's not exactly the mothering type." He heaved a sigh. "I thought you and Deb could work together."

"Why would I want to work with a home wrecker?"

Hearing those words spoken about his wife, he cringed. Yes, the circumstances surrounding his relationship with Deb were less than ideal, but he never viewed her as someone responsible for the end of his marriage. How could he get Stephanie to share his point of view? Knowing he couldn't, he shuddered. "For Adam's sake," he pleaded. "For my sake." His voice cracked at the end.

"I need to talk to my agent and the show's producer to see if they can write me out of the season or hire a replacement."

"Make it quick." Pressure built behind his eyes. "I start treatment on Monday."

"As soon as I have an answer, I'll call you."

A flurry of voices muffled in the background.

21

"I have to go," she said. "Thanks for telling me what's happening." A moment of silence bubbled between them. "I love you."

The shock of those three words hit his solar plexus. "You what?"

The dial tone beeped. She ended the call before he could respond.

The echo of those tender words danced in the shimmering heat. He didn't know what to feel. He hadn't thought much about her over the years. Why should he? He was happily remarried to the love of his life. He only married Stephanie because she was pregnant and wanted the child. He believed they could make a family. For twenty or so years, they hobbled along until Deb returned to Vine Valley to care for her sick mother.

Seeing Deb again, the girl he always admired from afar, rekindled his high school crush. His feelings for Deb flared out of control, destroying the family he created. His relationship with Stephanie ended, except for their brief interactions regarding Adam. He never imagined his ex-wife might still love him, especially after a six-month court battle over custody, finances, and the house he inherited from his parents. In the end, she left Vine Valley with only a box of clothes.

Turning the key in the ignition, he backed up the truck and headed home. The scent of the redwood trees permeated the thick, hot air. He rolled up the windows and turned on the air-conditioner, thinking of Stephanie. If the situation was reversed, he could not imagine shutting down his construction company and moving to Los Angeles. But here she was, prepared to rearrange her life and postpone her career to care for

Adam. His stomach twisted with regret. Maybe he should have given her more in the divorce. Maybe the vases she wanted that Deb just boxed up and stored in the attic after they married. Maybe the photo of Adam on her hip after she shot her first commercial in San Francisco or the photo from their wedding day in the backyard of his parents' home, her belly swelling beneath the white gown. He steered onto his street. The rows of identical houses provided a backdrop of comfort. Should he finally make amends with the woman whose heart he broke?

****

Deb sat in the dim light of Wine and Paint, waiting for Geraldine and Hope. Every Thursday was ladies' night out. She twirled the stem of her wineglass, and the scent of plums and blackberries elicited memories of when the group patronized Jasper's Bar and Grill. A sour taste filled her mouth. She set aside the glass before picking it up again for a quick sip of the tangy wine. How dare he invade her privacy at church this morning? Didn't he understand no one wanted to talk with him because of how he seduced Geraldine?

Sighing, she gazed across the crowded room full of the chatter and laughter of others. Some part of her didn't want to drink or paint. The other part of her needed ladies' night out more than ever. With the events of the past twenty-four hours still heavy on her shoulders, she slumped on the stool facing the blank canvas.

"Why so glum, sugar?" After a quick once-over, Geraldine frowned. She plopped her big, canvas bag to the left of Deb and slipped onto the stool.

She wore a pink tank top, khaki shorts, and kitten

heels. Her golden, cotton-candy-like hair framed her delicate features, from her perceptive blue eyes to her genuine smile. Deb grabbed the wine glass and twirled the stem in her fingers. She wanted to wait for Hope to arrive, so she could tell them the news together.

"Sorry, I'm late." Hope breezed through the crowd and claimed the seat on Deb's other side. When she gathered the long, caftan skirt around her legs, the metal bracelets on her wrists jangled. "The meeting with the tribe ran over, and I stayed to read Charlie's energy." She paused, meeting Deb's gaze. "Oh, dear, not you, too."

Her friend's concern plunged like a rock to the bottom of her stomach. How did Hope always know what was wrong before she told her? "I'm fine, really." She waved a hand. "But Cassidy's not." She gulped a mouthful of the dark, fruity wine for courage and set the glass on the table. "He has throat cancer."

Gasping, Geraldine threw her arms around Deb and tugged her close. "How terrible, sugar."

Deb breathed in the scent of pepper and gardenias dusting Geraldine's shoulders. She imagined her friend cooking dinner for her husband, Lionel, and watering the garden before slipping out for the night. She closed her eyes and held her friend closer. "I'm scared."

"Of course, you are." Geraldine released her and squeezed a hand.

The touch was warm, comforting, and full of strength.

"We'll support you in any way we can."

Nodding, Deb swiveled toward Hope. She stared into the fathomless eyes of her medicine woman friend, wondering what else Hope already knew. Like Deb, she was religious, but she called God the Great Spirit. Unlike Deb, she didn't kneel in a church pew or recite prayers along the beads of a rosary. Instead, she lay in a copse of redwood trees and listened to the sounds of nature.

"Don't worry." Hope smiled. "He'll be all right. The Great Spirit is with him."

"Are you sure?" Doubt prevented her from believing.

Hope adjusted the gown across her legs. "Sometimes a health crisis is a spiritual passage." She pursed her lips. "Cassidy has some growing up to do."

A server strolled by with a tray of chardonnay and cabernet sauvignon. A young man, he had a dimpled smile and wore his blond hair slicked back. He dressed in a white button-down shirt with a black bow tie and slim black slacks. "The artist is running late tonight, ladies. We'll start painting in fifteen minutes."

Geraldine grabbed two glasses of chardonnay and handed one to Hope. "The Great Spirit better be right. We're all too young to be dying."

"I agree." Deb curled her shoulders and stared into the depths of her wineglass. "But I can't stop thinking about my mom dying of cancer. I don't want to lose Cassidy. We've only been together a handful of years." She took a sip, then a gulp. The tangy fruit coated her throat and warmed her stomach. She pinched the stem of the glass between her fingers and blinked. "If you've read the Bible, you know God can be angry and vengeful. I don't want to be punished for breaking my vows and leaving the convent." She tipped back the glass, finished the wine, and set the empty glass on the counter. "Why can't He pick on me? Why hurt

25

Cassidy?"

"Because He knows Cassidy is the one you left Him for, sugar." Geraldine shook her finger. "He's a cuckold like Lionel. Only I returned to Lionel, and we reconciled. Weekly couples' therapy sure helped." She took a sip of wine and smiled. "We're renewing our vows in Vegas after the World Masters this September. I hope Cassidy will be well enough for you both to attend."

A tingle of surprised danced through Deb's body. She hugged Geraldine. "What great news!" A swell of happiness filled her chest. "Congratulations." A sinking feeling plunged through her center with the reality of her situation. "I don't know if we can go to Vegas. Cassidy has twelve weeks of radiation and chemotherapy ahead. He might not even finish playing the season."

"Don't worry. The team will find a replacement pitcher." Geraldine tapped her chin. "Maybe we can ask John."

Flinching, Deb widened her eyes. "Stephanie's brother?" From Cassidy, she knew all about the rivalry going back to high school. Even though Cassidy was the better player, he was benched for being the only freshman on the varsity team. Having John pitch in Cassidy's place would only bring up old wounds. "Can't you find another pitcher?"

Geraldine shrugged. "We'll see."

"Who knows?" Hope smiled. "Maybe Cassidy can finish the season."

The artist rushed into the room, her arms laden with supplies.

She was a small woman, dressed in a smock and

baggy pants with wild, gray-streaked hair.

"My apologies. Traffic was bad on the 101." She dumped her bags on the counter facing the group of men and women drinking wine. "Give me five minutes to set up, and then we'll paint this beauty." She held up a canvas showcasing a sunset over the ocean.

A gasp of appreciation rippled throughout the room.

Deb stared at the flaming orange rays against the blue waves and thought of the honeymoon to Hawaii she and Cassidy never took. A flash of anger shot down her arms and laced her hands into fists. Stephanie had called two days before Deb's wedding. She was offered a part in a movie. Filming started the following week. Could Cassidy take Adam for six months? Stephanie promised to care for him afterward. Without consulting Deb, Cassidy had agreed.

The bitterness and resentment of that decision churned Deb's stomach, and she grabbed the fullest glass of cabernet sauvignon from a passing server and gulped a mouthful to quell the rising fury. Between that woman's selfishness and Cassidy's complete devotion to Adam, Deb missed out on a tropical getaway. She huffed, tasting the bittersweet dregs of wine on her tongue. Cassidy was always making sacrifices for Adam. Why wouldn't Stephanie?

Chapter Four

On Saturday morning, Cassidy stepped onto the pitcher's mound and tugged the Crushers hat over his curls. Already the sun broke through the cloud cover, warning of another hot, summer day. He cupped the softball in his hand, his fingers caressing the rough stitching, while he waited for the team to line up for batting practice. After several upcoming tournaments in Northern California, the Vine Valley Crushers would head to Sacramento for the National Senior Softball Tournament to see which team would represent the West Coast in the World Masters Senior Softball Tournament in Las Vegas. For the past four years, the team battled well throughout the season but lost the chance to fight for the title. This year, the team was undefeated. Cancer-willing, he hoped for a chance to play in the finals and win the coveted title in September.

"I'm ready." Nick Gold, Jr., right fielder and home run hitter, stooped over home plate with the bat high over his shoulder. "Bring the heat."

Since high school, a carefree freedom enveloped Cassidy while he was on the pitcher's mound. No worries of his body, his life, or the future troubled him. He gripped the ball loosely in his left hand and, as always, brought the ball into the right-hand glove before beginning his pitch. With a smooth motion, he bent his knees just a little bit before dropping his left hand to the side and slightly behind his hips. Stepping forward with his right foot, he released the ball in an underhand motion.

With a quick swing, Nick hit the ball. A loud crack reverberated across the field, and the ball rocketed over the fence.

"Romeo!" Lionel cupped his hands around his mouth and strode out of the dugout. "What do you think you're doing?"

"I'm pitching." Cassidy grabbed a new ball from the bucket of balls beside the pitching net. Why was Lionel complaining? No one else on the team could pitch like he did. "What does it look like I'm doing?"

Lionel jerked a thumb toward the bleachers. "Get off the field."

Narrowing his eyes, Cassidy flung off his glove and spat in the dirt. "Why?"

Lionel stopped two feet in front of him and broadened his stance. "You can't play with cancer."

Nick jogged over. "What's going on?"

Realization bloomed in Cassidy's mind. *Deb must have told her friends on Thursday.* "Don't believe anything your wife says." A bristle of irritation traveled up his arms. Bending, he snatched his glove off the grass. "I intend to pitch as long as I'm able."

Lionel shook his head. "Not on my watch."

"You can't bench Cassidy." Frowning, Nick glanced between the two men. "Who will pitch for us?"

"John will." Lionel folded his arms over his chest. "He's itching to play."

Cassidy narrowed his gaze. "I bet." That man couldn't resist showing him up, not in high school and not in senior softball. "I can outpitch him any time. Cancer or no cancer."

Nick jabbed Cassidy's shoulder. "*You* have cancer?"

The concern in Nick's blue eyes cut through him. Heat flamed his face. "Yeah, I do." After a glance around the field, he lowered his voice. He didn't want the rest of the teammates to overhear him. "Throat cancer. I start treatment on Monday."

Nick leaned closer. "Do you need someone to drive you?"

"No, thanks. Deb will take me." Cassidy frowned. After she witnessed her mother's health deteriorate week after week from chemotherapy until she died, his wife was skittish about the idea of accompanying him to treatment. But, right now, she agreed to take him. He threw open his arms. "I'm fine, guys. I want to play as long as my body will allow, okay?"

Lionel spat in the dirt. "You don't run this team. I do." He thumbed his chest. "I'll be the judge of whether or not you play."

Gulping, Cassidy stared into the captain's steely, brown eyes. Lionel was a fair man and a good leader, but he was also cautious and caring. No player tested his physical limits whenever Lionel was around. Why get hurt if backup players were available?

"I'm the best pitcher this team's ever had." Cassidy straightened his lips. A scout for the major leagues spotted him during college and offered him a contract to play for the San Francisco pro baseball team. Bile flooded his mouth. If he hadn't turned down that offer, he wouldn't be here in a lousy T-shirt and shorts practicing slow pitch softball with a bunch of men over fifty. He would be retired from a career in the major leagues. Who knows? Maybe he would have won a World Series or two and been nominated for the Hall of Fame. He swallowed and winced from the pain.

Sadness clouded his thoughts. If he had accepted that offer, he would have left Stephanie, pregnant with Adam. He would have missed his son's first smile. He would have been unaware of the countless doctor's appointments and therapies as the experts scrambled to come up with a plan to help his son function beyond the limits of mild cerebral palsy and severe autism. He didn't regret his decision, but he didn't want to be asked to give up senior softball. Not for anything or anyone, especially not cancer. He widened his stance, bracing for resistance. "Just let me play, LJ." He hitched a breath, and his voice broke. "I need something to look forward to other than staying home and staring at the four walls."

Lionel glanced up and down the length of Cassidy's body. "Okay, you can play." He narrowed his eyes and shook a finger. "But Geraldine will kill me."

Chuckling, Cassidy punched Lionel's shoulder. "I'll tell Deb to keep Geraldine off your back."

"Promise?" Lionel removed his cap and scratched his head.

Surely, Geraldine would understand if Deb explained the situation. Cassidy widened his smile. "Promise." But would cancer let him play?

****

Every Saturday morning, while Cassidy attended batting practice, Deb stayed home to care for Adam. If she was lucky, she might wake early to enjoy a hot cup of coffee and the newspaper. Those conditions only happened if Adam slept through the night. Most of the time, he didn't. During those times, she was jostled awake by the sound of a cow bell clanging against the wall.

Adam slapped his feet against the hardwood floor, wandering down the hall and into the kitchen, searching for breakfast.

With her heartbeat lurching in her chest, Deb tossed aside the covers, shoved her feet into slippers, grabbed her robe, and cinched it across her waist. She scrambled out of the bedroom, jogged down the hallway to maneuver her way around Adam, and blocked the entrance to the kitchen to avoid another refrigerator raiding.

This morning Adam hadn't woken until after Cassidy returned from practice.

But Cassidy disappeared into the bathroom to shower and change, leaving Deb with breakfast duty. After popping frozen waffles into the toaster, Deb brewed a pot of coffee.

Adam sat at the kitchen table, flapping his hands and rocking back and forth, listening to the last strains of a guitar riff from the computer tablet.

With one hand carrying the coffee for her and the other hand carrying the plate of maple-syrup drenched waffles for him, Deb sat beside Adam to feed him breakfast.

Ten minutes later, across the room, Cassidy's phone rang on the kitchen counter.

She spooned the last waffle into Adam's mouth and frowned. *What's taking Cassidy so long?* Water plunked through the pipes in the wall. She grabbed the empty plate, strode to the sink, and washed her hands.

The phone kept ringing.

Craning her neck, she glanced at the caller ID. *Stephanie Burke.* She sucked in a sharp breath. *Why was Cassidy's ex-wife calling?*

With a damp paper towel, she wiped the sticky sweetness from Adam's mouth before she selected a new song from the computer tablet. A drum solo pounded from the tiny speakers.

Adam snatched the computer tablet out of her hands and hugged it to his chest. He wriggled out of the seat and wobbled down the hallway toward his room. The bedroom door clicked shut.

Cassidy's phone was silent for a few seconds before it trilled again.

With a glance, she confirmed the caller. *Stephanie Burke.* A bristle of irritation zigzagged up her spine. *Why couldn't she leave a message like anyone else? Did she think Cassidy was at her beck and call now that she was a Hollywood star?* With an angry flourish, Deb grabbed the phone off the counter, swiped her finger across the screen, and placed the phone against her ear. "Hello?" She held her breath, her pulse beating in her throat.

"Hi, this is Stephanie." A moment passed. "Deb?" Without waiting for a response, she continued. "Is Cassidy around? I need to speak with him."

The walls shuddered into silence. Deb glanced down the hall. Cassidy might have finished his shower, but he was not dressed. She wrapped an arm around her waist and leaned against the quartz counter. "He's not available. May I take a message?"

"Yes, you may." A moment of silence lapsed. "Tell him I won't be filming this season. I'm on my way to

Vine Valley. When I arrive, we can discuss Adam's care."

Adam's care? Frowning, Deb stood upright and shoved back her shoulders. "What do you mean?"

"Hasn't he told you?"

The exasperation in Stephanie's voice was palpable.

"You honestly don't expect him to change diapers during chemo, do you?"

Deb gasped. Why did Cassidy tell Stephanie about his cancer diagnosis without consulting her first? She stiffened and gripped the phone tighter. "We'll manage just fine on our own." She gritted her teeth. "You don't need to take time off from work."

"Well, I took off the season. And I expect to see Cassidy after I arrive in town. I'll text him details. Ciao."

Ciao? Who said ciao? Only a pretentious snob. Deb shuddered. "Goodbye, Stephanie." She stabbed the red button and tossed the phone on the counter. Frustration drained from her arms and pooled in her legs. *Why did he want help from Stephanie?* A rod of anger shot up her spine. She could hire extra help, if needed. Couldn't she? Closing her eyes, she clutched her roiling stomach. A litany of thoughts marched through her mind—home health care workers and hospice workers. Plus the additional care needed for Adam—behavioral specialists and in-home support services. Emotion welled up within her, threatening to topple her. *Oh, God, I can't go through this ordeal again. Once, with my mother, was enough.*

A cheerful whistle blew through the kitchen. She opened her eyes.

Cassidy ruffled a towel through his dark, sandy curls. "Hey, love, why the frown?"

Deb glowered at the phone on the counter.

"Who called?"

"Stephanie." Deb huffed, dropping her arms to the sides. "She's coming to town and wants to see you to discuss Adam's care."

He wrinkled his forehead. "Is she taking a break from filming?"

"No, she's taking off the entire season." Deb spread her arms wide. "Why didn't you tell me you contacted her?"

"Why did you answer my phone?" A vein throbbed in his neck. He seized the phone off the counter and shoved it into the front pocket of his khaki shorts. "I'm sick. I need help."

Deb jabbed a thumb at her chest. "I'll take care of everything. Not her." She pointed toward his pocket. "Don't bring your ex-wife into this situation."

"I had to inform her." Cassidy raked his fingers through his curls. "We share a child together."

Shaking her head, Deb waved a hand between them. "We share a life together. I don't want her coming between us."

"She won't. She's here for Adam's sake." He heaved a sigh, dropping his shoulders. "Who knows? You might need a break. You can't take Adam to Thursday nights with the girls."

"The girls can come over and help me with Adam." She folded both arms over her chest.

Tossing back his head, he chuckled. "Look at you tantruming like Adam." He slung the towel over a shoulder and grabbed her waist, tugging her close.

"Don't be so upset."

His mouth breathed warm air against her ear. She softened her shoulders and leaned against his solid chest. Closing her eyes, she listened to his heartbeat. How much longer would she hear that familiar rhythm?

"I'm sorry I didn't tell you I called her." He kissed her forehead. "I already told my crew at work. I also told the guys today at softball practice." He rubbed his nose against the nape of her neck. "Please forgive me for not keeping you informed."

Twisting out of his comforting embrace, she opened her eyes and gaped. "You can't play softball."

He shrugged. "Lionel is okay with me playing as long as my body lets me."

"I'm not okay with that arrangement." She shook her head, knotting her hands into fists. "Don't you remember how weak my mother was? She slept twenty hours a day seven days a week."

"And she was twenty years older than I am." With a fist, he thumped his chest. "I'm not letting this disease slow me down. I have a life to live."

"Maybe you'll have to put that life on pause for three months if you want to live longer." She choked on a gasp. After turning toward the sink, she grabbed a glass out of the cupboard and filled it with cold water. She gulped one mouthful after the next. The cool liquid soothed her nerves.

"How many times do I have to tell you I won't die?" He cupped her shoulders and massaged his fingers into the hard muscles.

The knots loosened slowly, and calmness unspooled throughout her body. She set aside the empty glass and gripped the edge of the sink with both hands, staring at their reflection in the glare of the window.

He kneaded her muscles like stiff dough.

Dropping her head to her chest, she closed her eyes and breathed in deeply. Maybe he was right, and he wouldn't die. Maybe, just maybe, she would have him a little bit longer.

Chapter Five

On the night before Cassidy started chemotherapy, he slipped into the master bedroom and shut the door.

Deb jerked her head and dropped the rosary beads on the mattress where she knelt praying.

After all this time, he still marveled at his wife's startled, brown doe-eyes and short, brown pixie hair. She looked like a surprised fairy with a beaded lasso. He knelt beside her and rubbed his lips against her bare neck. "Adam's finally sleeping." For thirty minutes, he curled next to his son on the twin mattress, holding him close until his shoulders relaxed and his breathing deepened. "We have a few minutes before he wakes asking for waffles or juice."

"Mmm…" She melted against the heat of his affection. "Let me just finish praying."

He stood, tugging her hand.

Sighing, she rose and tucked the rosary in a pouch on the nightstand.

Bending, he wrapped an arm under her knees and lifted her. Strength jolted out of his legs, and he quickly tossed her onto the silky sheets and covered her with his body.

She wrapped her arms around his neck and closed her eyes. Tears leaked beneath her lashes.

He kissed her salty cheeks. After slipping the straps of her nightgown over her shoulders, he traced his lips across her collarbone while his calloused hands caressed her curves. Pent-up love and frustration pulsed in his fingertips.

Shuddering, she bent back her head and arched her spine.

With each tender stroke, he wanted to make her feel safe and protected. How could he preserve the fragile joy of their lovemaking when nagging worry over the months ahead loomed like a shadow?

****

On Wednesday morning, after Deb escorted Adam onto the bus for adult daycare, she drove Cassidy to the hospital for his first round of chemo. Cassidy's appointments on Monday and Tuesday—to install a feeding tube and fit a shield to protect his face during radiation treatments—had been uneventful. Both times she sat in the waiting room, praying the rosary and tapping a foot against the linoleum floors.

This morning, as soon as she stepped into the hospital lobby, the stench of disinfectant roiled her stomach. She wrapped her arms around her waist and held her breath. *Don't get sick.* The white light above an elevator glowed, and the doors opened. "Ready?" She searched her husband's face.

He nodded, grabbing her hand and stepping into the small cavity.

The heat of his skin boosted her strength. Encapsulated in the tiny space, she leaned against the wall during the brief ascent. The elevator jerked to a stop at the seventh floor, and the doors parted. She stepped into the long, narrow hallway, and a flash of memories zipped through her mind—her lower back straining as she steered her mother in a wheelchair, the helpful nurses with tense smiles assisting her in transferring her mother from the wheelchair to the black recliner, the four-hour-long wait as fluid dripped into a port, her mother's half-closed eyes staring at the mindless flicker of the silent TV, and her own hands numb from worrying her rosary beads.

The infusion room was exactly as she remembered—cold, white, and full of patients lying on black recliners with their arms extended beside them. A receptionist sat at a desk, *clacking* away at a computer keyboard. Two nurses circled the room, tucking blankets around legs and filling plastic cups with water. Pressure built up behind Deb's eyes.

"Don't worry." Smiling, he squeezed her hand.

Tears escaped down her cheeks and dripped off her chin. She hitched her breath, released his fingers, and swiped her face with the back of her hands. "I'm sorry, but I can't go through this again." Pain twisted her insides, and she stumbled out of the room.

"Deb!"

His voice trailed after her. She darted into the nearest restroom and closed the door of the first vacant stall. Kneeling, she heaved up breakfast. A sour taste lingered on her tongue, and her throat burned. *Jesus, Mary, Joseph, pray for us*. She gasped, standing on quivering legs. After flushing the toilet, she unlocked the stall and splashed cold water on her burning face. She tugged back the heavy door, and her sneakers squeaked on the linoleum floors.

Her husband leaned against the wall, his hands shoved into pockets. "I called Nick. He's on his way." He pushed off on his heels and strode toward her. "You don't have to wait. You can go home."

Staring into his hazel eyes, her throat closed and her heart opened. "I'm-I'm sorry."

"Don't cry." He wrapped his arms around her waist and held her close. "I understand."

He smelled of citrus and sunshine, and not chemicals and death. Closing her eyes, she exhaled. "I wish I was stronger."

"I know you do."

He sounded patient, as patient as he was with Adam. She buried her nose against his shoulder and wondered if she was being childish. Shouldn't her faith be enough to banish her fears?

Chapter Six

"I'm here."

The sonorous voice roused Cassidy from a light slumber. Blinking, he met Nick's kind and gentle gaze. The familiar sky-blue eyes and broad smile warmed him more than the blanket covering his legs. Even before marrying Hope, Nick embraced life with a calm, logical demeanor tempered by the generosity of his heart. He was someone Cassidy could both rely on and trust. "Thanks for coming on such short notice."

"No problem." Nick shivered, crossed his arms over his chest, and rubbed his hands up and down the length of his biceps. "Feels like a freezer."

Cassidy chuckled. He usually ran hot, even in winter.

A nurse stopped by and handed Nick a blanket. "Lower temperatures aid in the treatment." She pointed toward his suit. "Next time wear sweats."

"Or a ski suit." Nick draped the blanket over his shoulders and huddled next to Cassidy. "How are you holding up?"

"Fine, I guess." Cassidy shifted on the black recliner, careful not to disturb the drip attached to the port in his upper chest. "Deb's taking things worse than I am. She threw up before I called you."

"No kidding?" Nick scrunched his forehead. "Did you tell Stephanie?"

From his pocket, Cassidy's cell phone trilled.

Another nurse frowned. "All phones are supposed to be turned off." She held out her hand and wiggled her fingers.

Tilting his hips, Cassidy withdrew the phone and stared at the screen. "Well, speak of the devil." He glanced at the nurse. "My ex-wife is calling. I need to speak with her."

"Later." She snatched the phone out of his hand and switched off the power. "Call her back in a few hours."

Nick laughed. "I'll keep his phone safe." With an extended hand, he accepted Cassidy's phone and tucked it into his breast pocket. "So, let's move on to estate planning. Have you given it any thought?"

Estate planning. Cassidy frowned. "I don't plan on dying."

"No one does. But if you do, who will take care of Deb and Adam?" Nick tugged the blanket toward his chest. "Do you have a life insurance policy? Or a special needs trust?"

A current of frustration flowed through Cassidy. He didn't have anything beyond his construction business and the tiny tract home he inherited from his parents' and retained in his divorce. Nick, on the other hand, was the richest man in Vine Valley. He lived in a mansion he inherited from his father on Wapi Mountain. Shaking his head, Cassidy sighed. "No, I don't."

"Let me set you up with both." Nick removed a small notepad and pen from his breast pocket. "I'll have an attorney draft the special needs trust for Adam, and I'll fund the first hundred thousand."

"No, please, don't." Cassidy glowered, curling his fingers into tight balls. "I invited you to keep me company and drive me home, not donate your services and money."

Nick scribbled some notes. "Deb doesn't work. Adam's disabled. Life insurance will provide a buffer because a reverse mortgage only goes so far." He tapped the tip of the pen against the notepad. "But I'm more concerned about Adam. He can't inherit any money directly without losing services." He lifted the pen and widened his eyes. "Maybe I should talk to Stephanie. Make her aware of what I'm doing and see if she has any input."

"No way." Frowning, Cassidy uncurled his hands and slapped the arms of the recliner. "You're not talking to my ex-wife."

Winking, Nick patted his breast pocket. "Her phone number's right here."

Not appreciating the sense of humor, Cassidy stretched out his arm. "Give me back my phone."

Nick grinned, lurching out of reach. "So, your phone's not password protected?"

A jolt of frustration bolted through him. Why protect his phone with a password? A wave of fatigue crashed through him. He slumped back in the recliner and flicked his wrist. "All right, you win." A spike of fear infused him with new energy. He leaned forward. "But Deb and I need to be present."

"Of course." Nick stood and removed the blanket, folding it neatly and setting it on the chair. "I'll be right back. I need to make a few calls."

As soon as he left, Cassidy wriggled his head back and forth against the recliner and groaned. What a mess! He didn't want Deb and Stephanie arguing about Adam's care, and he didn't want to plan for a future that didn't include him. But if he left everything to chance, what were the odds of no regrets?

****

After leaving Vine Valley Hospital, Deb stopped by St. Peter's Church to gather the linens used on the altar during the weekend masses. She strode into the dark nave, dipped her fingers into the cool, holy water, and made the sign of the cross. After turning to the left, she strolled into the sacristy. The small, windowless room at the back of the church was a toaster oven.

The door creaked open, and a middle-aged priest wearing a black cassock strode into the room.

"Good morning, Father Anthony." Deb smiled.

"Good morning to you, too, Mrs. Burke." He nodded, pivoting toward the closet where the vestments hung. "I'm presiding over a funeral today. Mr. Salazar passed away last weekend." He slid the hangers across the wooden beam, searching for the correct ceremonial robes.

A tightness squeezed across her chest. Although the parish was small, Deb didn't know Mr. Salazar. He attended the Spanish-speaking mass at seven-thirty, and she attended the nine o'clock English-speaking mass. She placed a hand on her empty stomach. The thought of death, once abstract, then in high relief with her mother's passing, glowed with neon clarity since Cassidy's diagnosis. Biting her lower lip, she grabbed the laundry basket full of soiled cloths and hugged it to her chest. "I hope his soul rests in peace, and his family is consoled."

Without turning to meet her gaze, Father Anthony

nodded. He slipped the purple gown over his head and adjusted the fit over his shoulders. "He was a faithful man, and so is his family. I'm certain God will take care of them during their mourning." Pivoting, he grinned. "What do you think?" He opened his arms wide and rotated like a doll in a musical jewelry box.

Purple, the Catholic Church's color of penance, preparation, and sacrifice, was also the color of the Vine Valley Crusher's jersey. Deb glanced away, eager to escape the claustrophobic room shrinking with each breath. "You look fine."

"Shall I wear the white or the black stole?" He held up two long scarves.

She glanced back and forth between the white for glory and the black for mourning. Shouldn't she choose the glory of the afterlife instead of dwelling on the mourning of those left behind? The walls of the room wavered. "Wear the white." She thrust her chin toward the stole.

Frowning, Father Anthony lowered his arms. "Are you okay?"

She set the laundry basket on the wooden bench between them. "My husband has cancer." Sinking onto the bench, she covered her face with both hands.

"Oh, Deb, I'm so sorry."

His shoulder leaned against her body. She could smell his aftershave. "Some part of me feels like God is punishing me for what I did."

"God doesn't punish," he said. "He forgives."

She lowered her hands and lifted her chin. "I don't think I've forgiven myself."

"What better time than now?" He stood before the mirror and adjusted the white stole.

46

Nodding, she stood and grabbed the laundry basket. Exiting the sacristy, she bypassed the fount of holy water and nudged against the heavy, wooden doors. Outside, lemon-yellow sunshine brightened the sky. Ruminating on past events, she steeled her back and stalked across the parking lot to the old sedan. Cassidy's marriage to Stephanie hadn't been perfect, or he wouldn't have pursued her. No matter how much she loved God, He would never shower her with hugs and kisses. With each step, she recalled the loneliness of her time at the convent, and more memories floated to the surface.

Smiling, she remembered falling in love with Cassidy for the second time. After grocery shopping, she had arrived at her mother's house. While placing each item in the refrigerator, she listened to a strong, baritone voice. Following the sound of recited poetry, she glimpsed Cassidy stooped in the bathroom, installing a walk-in tub. The poem he recited was one he wrote for her in high school. She lingered in the doorway. When he stood to retrieve some tools from his pickup truck, he accidentally brushed her arm. A spark of electricity split her open. Gazing into his hazel eyes, his breath soft and shallow, his scent feral and warm, how could she not embrace him? She hadn't expected him to respond, pinning her against the wall and kissing her all over, claiming her in a way God never had. She sighed. Why dwell on the bittersweet memories of the ties they both severed to unite with one another? Squinting against the sunlight, she popped open the trunk and set the laundry basket inside, desperate to release a weight much heavier than the one she carried.

Chapter Seven

"We need to talk." Cassidy stood beside the kitchen sink, staring at Deb. She could be praying with her head bent and her focus completely devoted to the plate encrusted with sticky syrup from the waffles Adam liked. He gripped the ledge of the quartz counter, his pulse quivering against his jaw. He planned his speech between Adam's departure for adult daycare and Deb's weekly trip to the church to deliver the clean linens for the weekend masses. He needed to tell her about his conversation with Stephanie and maybe even mention his talk with Nick about estate planning, but he feared a confrontation.

Deb turned off the faucet and dried her hands on a dishtowel. "Yes?"

The inscrutable look in her brown eyes softened his doubts. He dropped his hand to his side. "We need to meet with Stephanie."

"Why?"

Heat radiated from her body, and he involuntarily took a step back. He gulped. "I need help with Adam."

"No, you don't." Scowling, she wrung the dishtowel in her hands. "You're fine. You didn't throw up after chemo, and you didn't oversleep."

Frustration braided across his shoulders. How could he get her to see his point of view? He splayed his hands. "I don't want to change diapers in the middle of the night anymore."

"*I* can change diapers." She set aside the dishtowel and narrowed her gaze.

"What about tomorrow?" He lifted his arms. "I want to play in the tournament." If the team wanted to compete for the title in the World Masters, the team needed to stay in the hunt for the Western Champions. Did he need to remind her? He groaned. "We can't take Adam. He'll pull up the grass until he gets bored, then he'll tantrum."

Huffing, Deb folded her arms over her chest. "Are you sure you're well enough to play?"

He chuckled. "A moment ago, you said I'm fine."

She dropped her head and released her arms to the sides. "Okay, Stephanie can watch Adam this weekend."

A smile tugged at the corners of his lips. He wanted to ask her to go with him to Nick's house next week to discuss estate planning with Stephanie, but he didn't want to push his luck. One victory was enough for now. "Thanks." He touched her shoulder. "We'll have so much fun."

She lifted her head and stepped into his embrace. "I hope so."

He smiled and kissed the top of her head. "I promise." He glanced out the window into the backyard. The grass wiggled in the breeze. Fatigue trickled into his arms and legs with the thought of mowing the lawn. He buried his head against his wife's shoulder, smothering the worry. After all, he could hire a teenager for yard work. Right now, he needed to save his strength to pitch.

****

That evening, Deb assembled Adam's overnight bag. She hesitated for a long moment, wondering how many extra pajamas, T-shirts, and shorts she should pack for a weekend stay at Stephanie's brother's condo. From what she knew, Uncle John didn't have any extra clothing, but she couldn't confirm her suspicions. Better to err on the side of generosity. She selected one extra piece of each item of clothing from his dresser drawers.

Adam jabbed her shoulder. "Out."

She bristled, turning slightly to acknowledge his gesture. "As soon as I finish packing, I'll be out."

Adam grumbled and slammed the door against the wall. "Out!"

The knob dented the drywall. "Fine." Glowering, she zipped up the suitcase and stood. "I'll leave." She tugged the suitcase into the hallway.

He slammed the door.

Cassidy met her in the foyer. "Don't take it personally."

"Really?" She snarled, dragging the suitcase. She didn't want Adam to resent her for shipping him off for the weekend. After all, he wasn't used to spending much time with his mother, not with her working ten months out of the year. After releasing the handle, she slumped against the wall. "Why don't I stay and you go to the tournament? Lionel and Geraldine or Hope and Nick can take you."

He wrapped an arm around her waist and tugged her close. "I want to go with *you*."

Flattered by the notion, she smiled. But the reality of the situation settled like a stone between them. After stepping out of his embrace, she crossed her arms over her breasts. "I don't want Adam to hate me."

"He doesn't hate you. He hates the situation." He groped for her again.

She dodged him. "How can you be so sure?" A moment of hesitation fleeted across her husband's face, and she smirked. "You can't, can you?"

Outside, a horn honked.

"She's here." He strode toward the front door.

So soon. She braced her shoulders and gripped the handle of the suitcase.

"Stephanie, we're so glad to see you."

Deb winced, witnessing her husband embrace his ex-wife. How could he gush over her? A flare of jealousy ignited her skin. Sure, Stephanie was a stunner. With her long, red hair and flawless curves squeezed into a white tank top and denim shorts, she easily could be mistaken for a thirty-five-year-old nymph, and not the seventy-year-old hag she played on TV. Forcing a smile, Deb thrust out her other hand. "Good to see you again."

Stephanie stepped away from Cassidy and squeezed Deb's fingers. After a quick once-over, she widened her smile. "You're looking good, Deb."

Really? Deb flinched. She didn't dye her hair, get injections, have a tummy tuck, or a breast lift. How could she possibly look good by Hollywood standards? "I packed Adam's clothes." She wheeled the suitcase between them. "He's listening to his music in his room." She pointed toward the hallway.

Stephanie ignored the suitcase. She hooked a hand in the crook of Deb's arm and steered her out of the foyer and down the hallway. Bending, she tipped her mouth toward Deb's ear. "Is he drinking?"

The soft, breathy voice tickled her ear. She jerked her arm free and took a step back. "Why are you whispering?" The woman towered over her like a red-haired giant. She bristled. "I stopped buying beer."

Stephanie flicked her glance down the hallway before taking a step closer. "He's always been a heavy drinker. If he doesn't stop, he'll never get well."

Thrusting back her shoulders, Deb stood as tall as her petite frame allowed. She jutted her chin. "I trust he's following doctor's orders."

Stephanie pouted and touched Deb's shoulder. "Be a good wife and take care of him, will you?"

Be a good wife? Deb seethed, hating the false intimacy. *How dare she tell me what to do?*

Turning, Stephanie strode down the hallway. "Adam! Mommy's here."

The door to Adam's bedroom opened. "Mama!"

"I'm right here, baby. Mommy's come to take you for a little ride to Uncle Johnny's house."

Deb stood mutely in the hallway, stunned by the saccharine reunion and the insolence of Stephanie's words.

Adam flung his arms around his mom's neck and smiled. "Up!"

"No way, young man. You're big enough to carry me." She chuckled, stepping out of his clingy arms and grabbing his hand. "Let's get you into Uncle Johnny's truck, okay?"

"Go." He grabbed his shoes and handed them to Stephanie.

Tugging the suitcase, Deb stalked back into the foyer and flattened her lips.

"What's wrong?" Cassidy frowned.

Everything, Deb wanted to say, but she would be exaggerating. Bitterness clung to her tongue, and she swallowed the venom she wanted to speak. "He obeys her."

"He's just excited for a car ride." Cassidy touched her shoulder. "Doesn't mean he likes her better than you."

Adam darted ahead and sat cross-legged on the floor of the foyer.

Kneeling, Stephanie tied the shoes on Adam's feet. "Let's get your suitcase, okay?"

Deb rolled the suitcase toward Adam.

He lurched for the handle and wobbled out the doorway onto the porch. "Bye."

"Wait." Stephanie placed a hand on her son's shoulder. "Give your dad and Deb a hug, first."

Pivoting, Adam leaned his body toward his father first, then Deb. "Bye-bye." He tottered down the driveway where Uncle John's black pickup truck was parked.

Tinny drums pounded behind Deb. She gasped. *Adam's music*. Darting down the hallway, she stepped into his bedroom and searched for the location of the sounds. She found the coveted music beneath a pile of dirty clothes Adam had thrown from the hamper. She grabbed the computer tablet, scurried down the hall, and out of the house. The evening sun slanted across the driveway, casting long shadows against the pavement. "You forgot your music." She thrust the prized possession into Adam's hands.

Sitting in the backseat of the pickup, with his seatbelt strapped across his chest, he clutched the tablet and smiled. A string of guitar sounds whined from the speakers. "Thank you."

"You're welcome." Pride and love radiated from the center of her chest. Smiling, she kissed the top of his head, which smelled of her floral shampoo. "Have a good weekend with your mommy. See you on Sunday."

"Bye." He tugged the handle and shut the door.

"Good luck at the tournament." Stephanie hopped into the cab and started the engine.

"Thanks." Cassidy strolled over to Deb and grasped her hand. He nuzzled his nose against her ear. "You're a good stepmom."

His hot breath and kind words were comforting. She squeezed his fingers.

The truck backed out of the driveway and rolled out of the cul-de-sac.

With the weight of caring for Adam lifted, Deb leaned into her husband. "I try." Her efforts only mattered so much. After all, whether Cassidy lived or died, she would never be Adam's mother. The truth hurt like a jab to the ribs.

Chapter Eight

At the bottom of the open inning, the Vine Valley Crushers led twelve to eight against the Redwood City Robbers. Cassidy stood on the mound, fighting against an increasing fatigue that left his left arm weaker with each pitch. The Redwood City heat—dry and relentless—didn't help. He was thirsty, craving a cold beer, and not the iced water Deb packed in the cooler. After studying the batter, he took a step forward and lobbed a slow, underhanded pitch.

The batter swung the bat. The ball popped up and rocketed back down.

With a raised arm, the catcher grabbed the fly ball.

"Out!" The umpire waved a clenched fist.

The next batter shuffled to the plate. He bent at the waist and practiced a couple of swings before stepping into position.

Cassidy narrowed his gaze and tossed the ball. The arch of the throw was lower, and the ball barely traveled over home plate.

The batter swung and missed.

"Strike!" The umpire balled up his right hand.

Cassidy gnawed on his lower lip and kicked his feet in the dirt. *I'm losing power*.

"C'mon, Cassidy, give him the heater," Deb yelled from the bleachers.

Glancing to the left of home plate, he glimpsed his

wife sitting among her friends. When he glimpsed her smile, his confidence returned. *Just a couple of more throws, and this game will be over*. He cupped the ball in his glove for a moment before transferring it to his left hand and winding up for another pitch.

After stepping into the swing, the batter hit the ball, dropped the bat, and lunged into a run for first base.

From the infield, Nick caught the ball and threw it to Lionel, the first baseman, just a split second before the batter stepped on the bag.

"Out!" The umpire hammered his right fist.

In the stands, the Vine Valley Crush women cheered and clapped. "Whoo-hoo!"

Cassidy smiled, tugging his cap tight against his forehead. He spat on the ground and winced from a sharp pain in his throat. *Only one more out to go*.

"C'mon, Cass!" Deb shouted. "You can do it!"

The energy deflated from his body like helium leaking from a balloon. He folded at the waist, gasping for air. *Don't let your wife down. Don't let your team down*. After regaining his breath, he rose and cupped the ball in his glove. He eyed the batter, a short guy with a broad stance who kept the bat tight against his shoulder. After a long windup, Cassidy flung his wrist. The ball arced and landed a couple of inches before home plate.

"Ball." The umpire nodded.

Cussing beneath his breath, Cassidy bowed his head and focused. *Put a little more power behind the throw, and I'll only have to lob three more pitches*. He took a step forward and released the ball in a higher, longer arc.

The batter swung. A loud crack exploded against

the bat. The ball sailed over the fence.

Cassidy shook his head. *One run, two outs. Score is twelve to nine.*

"C'mon, Cass," Deb shouted. "Hold them."

But each subsequent pitch was sloppier and weaker than the previous one.

The batters responded with base hits.

Cassidy shifted his feet on the mound. He glanced over to the dugout, wondering if Lionel would call in John as the relief pitcher.

His ex-brother-in-law stood behind the cyclone fencing, intently watching the game.

The bases were loaded.

Cheers erupted from the other team's bleachers.

His wife and her friends stood and hollered. "Go, Cass! Go! Give him the heater."

He thought of the previous pitches. Sometimes the ball fell short and missed the plate. Other times the ball traveled exactly where he wanted it to go. The unevenness of his pitching troubled him. Fatigue tugged his arm muscles, and his breathing jagged his lungs. A prickling sensation traveled up his legs and lodged at the bottom of his spine. *Can I do this?* With his head bent, he glanced at the ball in his hand, then at the batter. He wound up and threw a high, underhanded pitch. Between a slightly off aim and a lack of force, the ball arched away from center and veered left toward the edge of the strike zone.

The batter swung. The ball cracked against the bat, ricocheting between first and second bases.

The players on second and third both crossed home plate.

The shortstop scooped the ball and tossed it to

Lionel at first base.

"Out!" The umpire clenched his fist.

The Vine Valley Crushers won the game twelve to eleven.

Cassidy tossed his glove into the air. "We won! We won!"

His teammates swarmed around him, patting him on the shoulder and high-fiving. But no matter how wonderful winning felt, deep down, he worried the exhaustion of his body meant the greater battle was lost.

****

Deb sat on a stadium cushion with her chin propped in her hands. The afternoon heat plastered her short hair to her forehead and the base of her neck. Every muscle in her body tensed. As soon as the umpire thrust his fist into the air announcing the final out, she jumped up. "They won!"

Geraldine gasped, clasping her hands over her mouth. "They sure did, sugar."

With a short exhale, Hope clapped her hands. "Well, that game was mighty close."

The tornado of worry spinning in Deb's mind finally calmed. She climbed down the bleachers.

"Where are you going?" Geraldine shouted.

"To the dugout." Deb wanted to congratulate her husband. She ran around the cyclone fence, ducked into the covered shelter, and bumped into someone. Glancing up, she recognized the shock of red hair sticking out of a cap, the freckles across the bridge of the nose, and the long, lanky body. "John." She hitched her breath and widened her eyes. "What are you doing here?"

"I'm the backup pitcher." He smiled, exposing the

dimple in his cheek. "Lionel thought the team might need help if Cassidy couldn't play." He pointed toward the field. "But he's playing better than ever."

Not really. Deb swallowed her fears. She wasn't about to let Stephanie's older brother and Cassidy's ex-brother-in-law know she doubted whether her husband could finish pitching the remaining three games this weekend. After all, John was Cassidy's rival from high school. When Cassidy was promoted as a freshman to the varsity team, he played backup pitcher to John. Cassidy didn't like it. He wanted to be the lead player, even if it meant starting with a lower division. The anger and tension plus the hurt feelings over the divorce bubbled between the two men, even now.

John thrust out a hand. "Good to see you."

"You, too," she lied. Dodging his hand, she stooped and opened the cooler.

"How rude."

His voice rubbed her skin like sandpaper. She flattened her lips in silence.

"I hope you're not this rude to my sister."

She flinched from the grating words. "I'm sorry if you think I'm rude, but I need to get Cassidy some water." She dug her hands into a puddle of sloppy, wet ice.

"Let me help you." He knelt and plunged his hand into the cooler, his fist emerging with a bottle of water. With one quick twist, he released the cap. "Here you go."

No tone of anger, sarcasm, or malice laced his voice. She froze, cradling the cold, moist bottle in her hand. "Thank you."

"You're welcome." He stood and removed his cap

to scratch behind an ear. "Stephanie and I lost our stepdad to cancer a year ago. She still feels bad she didn't take time off from filming to be there during his final days." He swallowed and glanced away. "We just want to help."

She clutched the bottle. Icy beads of water trickled down her fingers. He was right. A flush of guilt heated her cheeks. John didn't need to volunteer to be a backup pitcher, but here he was, ready to be of service. "I'm sorry I was rude."

"Apology accepted." He stepped aside and waved toward the field. "Go congratulate your hero."

With a sidelong glance, she nodded before darting onto the field with the water bottle lifted high above her head like a trophy.

Cassidy scooped her into his arms.

His grip was a loose lasso around her body. After a victory, he usually picked her up and swung her around in a circle until she giggled. But he couldn't lift her body anymore.

"I'm so proud of you." She offered him the water bottle.

He poured a mouthful, swallowed, and grimaced. Dribbles splashed down his chin.

Worry pummeled into her, and she stepped back. "Do you feel well enough to pitch the next game?"

Frowning, he rubbed the sweat off his forehead. "I don't know. I'm so tired."

Please, God, don't let him get weak and die like my mother did. Fear tightened all the muscles along her spine. She clenched her jaw. "Ask Lionel to bench you."

Widening his eyes, he gasped. "Why?"

After a glance at the dugout, she clutched his hand. "John's here as the relief pitcher."

He narrowed his gaze.

"I know you two have history, but I need you to look past the circumstances for once." She leaned closer. "His stepdad died of cancer last year," she whispered. "He wants to help. I think he's honest."

Jerking back, Cassidy flicked his gaze toward the dugout. "I don't know."

"Please." She wanted him to be safe and not sorry. "Just one game. You can pitch again tomorrow, if you feel well enough."

His gaze softened. "Okay." He squeezed her hand. "I'll ask Lionel to sit me for the next game, and we'll revisit the lineup tomorrow."

"Thanks." She kissed his cheek. "I love you."

"I love you, too." He strode out to center field where Lionel and the team gathered.

Clutching her hands to her chest, she hoped he would only have to sit out one game and be ready to play tomorrow.

Chapter Nine

The sun slanted across the field, casting long shadows against the bench where Cassidy sat in the dugout watching the final game of the day. A slight breeze wafted through the chain link fence, breaking up the monotony of sizzling heat. The team was playing against the Carson City Diggers, a tough win from his experience. If only he didn't feel so weak and tired. No longer working, no longer pitching, no longer parenting, he laced his hands between his knees and wondered what was left of his identity. The weight of each loss sagged against his sloped shoulders. Some part of him felt useless, as unnecessary as he was back in high school sitting in the dugout watching John pitch.

Leaning forward, he observed the game. The Crushers were up five runs against the Diggers. At the top of the third inning, he studied John on the pitcher's mound. He committed every microscopic movement to memory, from the way John cupped the ball to his gaze on the batter. Some part of him wanted John to fail and to prove Cassidy was the better pitcher, even if it cost the Vine Valley Crushers a tournament win. The other part of him simmered in the unwanted brew of thoughts about his health. For the first time since Adam's diagnosis as a baby, Cassidy felt powerless.

He glanced at his wife and her friends clustered on the bleachers beneath an awning. He felt as helpless as

Noelle, Geraldine and Lionel's old dog, lying in a cart, lifting her head every now and then to catch a glimpse of the goings-on. Maybe he should have stayed home. At least, in the quiet of the living room, he would have the company of Adam. The thought of his son squeezed his chest. How would Adam cope with Cassidy's permanent absence?

I'm not dying. With the team in the outfield, Cassidy eyed the cooler. Maybe he should have a beer—just one to help him stop thinking. The temptation lingered through the fourth inning. By the top of the fifth inning, he glanced at the bleachers to confirm the women were watching the game. With a quick flick of his wrist, he opened the lid, plunged his hand into the sloshing ice, and withdrew a can of beer. He cracked open the seal and gulped a mouthful of bitter fluid. The cold liquid scorched his throat and warmed his stomach. But the best part was his thoughts quieted to a low hum.

Much better. Relief loosened his shoulders. He finished the beer, crushed the can beneath his shoe, and tucked the evidence in his softball bag.

At the end of the inning, his teammates rushed into the dugout. They tossed aside gloves, picked up bats, and studied the lineup.

The chatter rose around him like a dust cloud, thick and annoying. Cassidy squinted, half listening, half drifting, not here or there, just lost in his misery. Out of the chaotic interlude, a voice rose in his mind. *Just one more.* He snuck a glance at the cooler, his hands sweaty, and his heartbeat skipping. *One more won't hurt.* Squinting, he searched the bleachers. Deb had left, probably to go to the restroom. Hope rested her chin in her hands, her gaze focused on the game. Geraldine bent to feed the dog sandwich scraps.

The team scored five runs during the next inning.

With a whoop and a holler, the teammates switched from offense to defense. Each player jogged to his position on the field.

"Don't let them score." Lionel cupped his hands around his mouth. "We can win this game!"

Bending, Cassidy stole another can of beer from the cooler. The crack of the seal, an illicit sound, triggered memories of seducing Deb for the first time in her childhood bedroom during her mother's illness. The rush of temptation and the fear of getting caught thumped wildly in his veins. He was alive, no matter what the doctor predicted of his future. With an empty stomach and only a bottle or two of water, the second beer shocked his body. All the edges of his skin blurred, and his tongue numbed. A satisfying haze descended on his mind, his thoughts gauzy wisps, as ephemeral as clouds in the sky. He leaned back on the bench, enjoying the game for the first time.

John wasn't a bad pitcher. Not bad at all. Maybe not as talented as Cassidy, but in a team game, no one player was significant. Cassidy crushed the can beneath his heel and tossed the silver, aluminum disc into his bag. He snuck a glance at the bleachers and plunged his hand into the cooler for a third beer, hoping he would not get caught.

****

After winning the final game of the day, the Vine Valley Crushers met at a local bar and grill for a celebratory dinner. Squinting, Deb stepped into the dark restaurant and shivered. The air-conditioner was set too low and so were the lights.

A hostess led the teammates to the banquet hall in the back.

Chandeliers fashioned out of wagon wheels hung from the ceiling, casting dim puddles of light against the dark, wood-paneled walls. Deb wove her way around the long, rectangular table and chairs dominating the space. Glancing over her shoulder, she witnessed Cassidy sway and stumble, grabbing the back of a chair for balance. *Is he drunk?* A flash of anger narrowed her gaze. *How dare he?* She turned and stepped closer, wanting to smell his breath. "Are you okay?"

Nodding, Cassidy raised a hand. "I'm fine."

He's lying. She grabbed his hand and took a seat in the middle of the long, rustic table. The hard back of the chair straightened her spine. She waited until he was seated beside her before she released his hand.

Nick pulled back a chair and sat, slapping his cap on the table. "How about I buy the team the first round of beer?"

A leap of panic jolted through her veins. *No beer.* Deb waved to the server. "Please bring us a few pitchers of water." Turning to her husband, she studied his drooping eyes and withered posture. *He looks tired.* She straightened her lips. "Are you sure you're up for a full meal with the team?" She leaned closer. Sniffing, she caught a whiff of his sour breath. Every muscle in her back stiffened. *Where did he get the beer?* She touched his wrist. "We can go back to the hotel and order room service."

"No." He heaved a sigh. "I'll be fine."

The rough edges of his voice sliced through her

concern. *Why bother to control him? If he wants to drink, he'll drink. How can I or anyone else stop him?*

The server delivered a pitcher of beer and a pitcher of water.

Deb filled a glass of water and placed it before Cassidy. "Have some water."

He glared at the glass.

She grabbed her purse, hooked over the back of the chair, and fished out her rosary. The beads in her dry hand soothed her. Bowing her head, she silently recited the prayers.

The rest of the teammates and their wives drifted into the room. Their loud banter and raucous laughs clashed like cymbals and drums.

Hope brushed by, placing a hand on Deb's shoulder. "May I sit next to you?"

The gentle tone in her voice reassured Deb. "Of course." She curled her lips into a smile and squeezed her friend's soft hand once before letting go.

A few moments later, Geraldine flopped into the chair across from Deb. "I told Lionel I'd go with him to take Noelle to the hotel, but he insisted on dropping me off first." She wedged her purse into the chair beside her. "I swear I didn't think we'd win that third game. Not with the way Lionel was hitting." She shook her head. "That arthritis of his keeps acting up. But he won't try acupuncture. He says needles are no better than voodoo." She shrugged. "Drugs don't always work, do they, sugar?" After placing her napkin in her lap, she poured a glass of water. "How's treatment coming along?" She widened her eyes at Cassidy.

"Okay. I guess." Cassidy sipped from the glass of water and winced. "I won't really know until the doctors take another PET scan four weeks after treatment ends just before Thanksgiving."

Geraldine winked. "Well, sugar, we'll have something to be thankful for, won't we?"

Deb hunched her shoulders and bit her lower lip. *How could Geraldine assume the best outcome?* She tucked her rosary in her pocket and rolled the silverware out of the cloth napkin. A fork, spoon, and knife clattered against the wood tabletop like coins dropping from a slot machine. She spread the cloth napkin over her sticky thighs. All she wanted was to skip this mandatory meal and take a hot shower before collapsing into bed with Cassidy for the night. She didn't know if he intended to play tomorrow, but she wanted to be rested.

The server delivered another pitcher of beer and another pitcher of water. A few moments later, the server returned with two baskets of bread and butter.

Geraldine grabbed the basket, broke off two slices, and slathered them both with butter. "Mmm-mmm." She nudged the basket toward Cassidy. "Still warm."

Cassidy fiddled with the loaf. Crumbs scattered on the table. He spread butter across the jagged piece before biting into it. Nodding, he chewed. "Good." He passed the basket to Deb.

Even surrounded by the comfort of friends, Deb couldn't eat with a churning stomach. She offered the bread basket to Hope.

"Are you okay?" Hope raised her eyebrows, accepting the basket.

"Not really." Deb glanced around the table at the teammates and their significant others. Cassidy had his head tilted toward Nick, the two of them engaged in a conversation.

"Want to talk?" Hope tore a piece of bread and placed the basket in the center of the table.

"Where?" Deb sighed, scanning the banquet hall.

Geraldine cleared her throat. "We can meet in the ladies' room, sugar, just like high school." She bit into her buttered bread and chewed.

"I'll leave first." Hope stood and smoothed her skirt with her hands. She wandered out of the room and turned right.

Deb waited a few moments after Geraldine left the table before she stood and touched Cassidy's shoulder. "I have to use the restroom. I'll be back in a little bit."

He cupped her hand with his fingers. "What shall I order for you if the server comes back?"

Thinking of her waiting friends, she shrugged. "Whatever you're ordering."

"Are you sure?" He furrowed his brow. "I'm ordering a side of steamed rice and vegetables, and not a main dish."

How could she forget? With his frequent nausea, he could only eat small, bland meals. She grabbed a menu off the table and scanned the entries. "Order the salmon with salad and blue cheese dressing." She placed the menu aside and forced a tight smile. She stalked down the hallway and shoved open the door of the ladies' room. Two stalls and one sink filled the tiny facility.

Geraldine stood before the mirror, fluffing her hair with her fingertips.

Hope leaned against the wall beside the paper towel dispenser.

The air stank of emptied bowels and cheap

perfume. Deb wriggled her nose. "Sorry I'm late. Cassidy wanted to order for me."

"Ah, sugar, you should have told him you wouldn't be gone long." Geraldine puckered and reapplied a pink gloss to her lips.

"What's bothering you?" Hope crossed her arms over her chest.

Deb heaved a sigh. "Cassidy's been drinking, and he's not supposed to."

"Where'd he get beer, sugar?" Geraldine swiveled the lipstick shut and shoved it into her purse. "He was in the dugout."

"The cooler." Deb remembered rooting around the assortment of bottles and cans. "I'm sure the guys have everything in there, booze included."

Hope frowned. "He doesn't seem impaired."

"You didn't witness anything because you arrived late, and I've been encouraging him to drink water." Deb threw open her arms, almost smacking both friends. "I don't want him to get any sicker. I can't afford to have him pass out. He needs to listen to the doctor and stay hydrated."

Geraldine stepped aside and shook her head. "Listen, sugar, you need to back off." She tore a sheet of paper towel and blotted her lips. "Remember when Michelle was pregnant, and Lionel wouldn't leave her alone, and I accused him of cheating?"

Deb nodded. Of course, she remembered. Every time Geraldine visited Deb's house, she complained.

"Well, once I stopped pestering him, he stopped seeing her."

"Not entirely true." Hope stepped forward. "He visits her baby three times a week."

Geraldine crumpled the paper towel into a ball and tossed it into the garbage can. "He babysits Mondays, Wednesdays, and Fridays, so she can work." She shoved back her shoulders and lifted her chin. "Sometimes I come along. We're godparents."

"What does any of this conversation have to do with Cassidy's drinking?" Deb glanced from one friend to the other.

Hope touched Deb's shoulder. "You can't control him. When Richard was sick—"

Richard? Heat flushed through her body at the mention of Hope's first husband who died from old age. *How dare Hope compare the two men?* She crumpled her face. "Cassidy is not Richard." Pressure welled in the backs of her eyes. "I don't care how you handled Richard's illness. He died." She shuddered, her voice rising. "I want Cassidy to live."

The door opened, and a woman wedged into the bathroom. "Are you all in line?"

"No, sugar." Geraldine ushered her friends between the sinks to make room. "You go ahead. We're having a talk."

The woman wove around the three friends and shut the door to a stall.

Hope motioned for them to exit into the hallway.

"I'm not ready to leave." Deb folded her arms over her chest. "You two can go ahead without me. I want to be alone."

"Are you sure?" Geraldine placed a hand on her hip and frowned.

Deb sniveled and rubbed the back of her hand under her nose. "I don't want to be a bad wife by letting him do whatever he wants to do."

"You're not a bad wife, sugar." Geraldine wrapped an arm around Deb's shoulders.

"Stephanie implied I was." The sour taste of failure lingered on her tongue. Deb leaned her head against Geraldine's shoulder.

Hope raised a fist. "Why are you listening to the ex-wife?"

"She knows him better than me. They were married for over twenty years."

"Time isn't everything, sugar." Geraldine rubbed a hand against Deb's shoulder. "Look at me and Lionel. Thirty years caused more problems than they solved." She released her friend. "If we didn't go to counseling, we wouldn't be together. Maybe you and Cassidy need to see a professional who can help you through this ordeal."

The toilet flushed, and the woman stepped out of the stall and washed her hands.

Hope passed the woman a couple of paper towels.

Geraldine held open the exit door.

The woman shuffled into the hallway.

As soon as the door closed, Deb pouted. "I don't know if Cassidy will agree to go to counseling. He said it didn't work the first time around."

"The first time around he was dating you behind his wife's back." Geraldine wagged a finger. "This time around he's flirting with cancer. I doubt he'll choose cancer over you."

Maybe. Maybe not. The illicit beers in the dugout and the sour smell on Cassidy's breath troubled Deb. She shuddered. What if the next time he drank, he didn't stumble into a banquet hall but fell and lost consciousness? Another pinprick of uneasiness lodged at the base of her spine. Hope's advice to let go of control didn't resonate with her. Neither did Geraldine's advice of couples' therapy. After opening the door, she stepped into the cool hallway. Comforting smells of roasted beef, split pea soup, and twice-baked potatoes wafted from the nearby kitchen. A low grumble erupted from the pit of her stomach. She wanted to give Cassidy his freedom. She also wanted to be a good wife. Why did one action cancel the other? In the banquet hall, she stalked toward the table.

Waving his broad hands, Cassidy was still talking with Nick.

If she peered closely, she could see the hollowness in his eyes. After taking a seat, she grabbed her glass of water and sipped the ice-cold liquid. When she placed down the glass, she noticed a pint of beer beside Cassidy's glass of water. Her stomach flipped. "Is that beer your drink?" She nudged Cassidy's shoulder.

Cassidy lowered his hands and frowned. "No, that beer is Nick's."

"Why is the glass next to *your* plate?" Deb jabbed a finger at the space between them.

"The table isn't big enough." Nick chuckled. "I'm sorry." He lifted the glass and took a sip.

"Relax." Cassidy grasped her arm and leaned forward for a kiss.

He tasted like bitter beer. Tension coiled in the back of her neck. Was Nick covering for him?

After glancing around the table at her friends, she decided not to make a scene. Instead, she wrapped her arms around Cassidy's neck and kissed him again. As she released him, she flashed a smile, pretending to be happy. Inside, she grumbled, not knowing what to do.

Chapter Ten

Weeks later, Cassidy sat on the examination table in Dr. Rodriguez's office. The blue paper hospital gown clung to his skin, and the blast of cold air from the air-conditioning vent quivered along his exposed legs. Strong scents of ammonia and bleach emanated from the surfaces of the tiny room. Clasping his hands in his lap and swinging his legs against the metal table, he waited.

Two knocks on the door preceded Dr. Rodriguez's entrance. "Good morning." She smiled, extending her hand. "How are you doing today?" She shook his hand firmly. The white lab coat was fully buttoned, but her long black hair swung loose down her back.

"Not good." Over the past three weeks, he lost ten pounds. The sores in his mouth proliferated, making eating and swallowing worse. He didn't want to use the feeding tube unless necessary. The task of hooking up the equipment and monitoring Adam so he wouldn't barrel through the living room and knock everything down wasn't worth the effort. But losing muscle strength and relentless fatigue weren't better options. As he headed into the fourth week of treatment, he hoped the doctor would have some good recommendations.

Nodding, she listened to his concerns. The crevice between her eyebrows deepened. "Let's take a look and see what's happening." She turned on the light of the otoscope. "Open, please." She pressed a wooden depressor against his tongue.

He gagged.

Frowning, she withdrew the instrument and typed some notes into his medical file. "Have you been eating anything spicy?"

"No." He swung his legs. The foods he ate consisted of bananas, applesauce, tofu, and rice—bland and tasteless.

"Fried?" She arched an eyebrow.

"No." He glanced down at his bare feet. Every day he drove by his favorite fast food restaurant, sniffing the onions rings, but he never stopped. The smell wafted through the air-conditioning vents and filled the truck with childhood longing. Whenever he received good grades or won a softball game, his parents treated him to a child's meal. They always paid extra to swap out the fries for onion rings.

"Any alcohol?" She bent over the keyboard, eyeing the screen.

He stiffened. Since he snuck three beers from the cooler at the softball tournament, he drank every day. After the bus picked up Adam for day care, he drove to the construction site of Larry's Deli to check with Guillermo about the progress. On his way home, he stopped by the convenience store and bought a six-pack of beer. He parked, sneaking his purchase into the garage, if Deb was home. On the days he was alone, he carried the beer into the kitchen and cracked open each can and drank until the walls of the room dissolved. He always smashed the cans and shoved them into a plastic bag, which he kept in the garage, before dumping them into the recycling bin. Dr. Rodriguez stood. "How much have you been drinking?"

"I'm not." A rush of heat invaded his face.

"Alcohol makes everything worse." She opened her arms to encompass the room. "First, alcohol inflames the liver. You'll have more side effects from chemotherapy." She lifted a hand and curled each finger toward her palm. "Nausea, vomiting, stomach cramps, and fatigue." She lowered her arm and tapped a foot against the linoleum. "Alcohol also irritates mouth sores, making them worse."

Cassidy gulped and flinched. "I'm not drinking."

She held his gaze.

The force of the lie felt like a palpable presence. He bowed his head and laced his fingers together in his lap.

"If you don't stop drinking, you'll either prolong treatment or die."

Die? He snapped his head and locked onto her gaze. "Dr. Prasad said throat cancer is very treatable."

Dr. Rodriguez stalked to the computer. The *click-clack* of her fingertips on the keyboard echoed in the room. "Dr. Prasad thought your throat cancer was caused by a virus, not alcoholism."

"I'm not an alcoholic." Cassidy scrubbed his face with his hands. "I only drink to take off the pressure just like everyone else."

"You're not everyone else. You're a cancer patient." Shaking her head, she continued typing. "You need to find another outlet for release. Long walks, hot baths, soothing music, lighthearted movies, or entertaining books are more effective. Some people find meditation or prayer to be helpful." She stopped typing and swiveled. "If you can't stop drinking on your own, you need to attend a support group for alcoholics or an outpatient treatment program, understand?"

He scrunched his shoulders toward his ears. "I promise I won't drink." When she stood, she loomed larger-than-life, an angry adversary in a white lab coat with a list of demands. Inside, he cowered into a small, helpless child. *Can I stop drinking?* The past replayed in his mind like a movie. Each scene featured footage from underage beer parties to collegiate booze fests to weekly gatherings with either his construction crew or softball team at the local bar. A hard lump settled at the bottom of his stomach. For the past forty years, alcohol was a part of daily life. He grimaced. What would he do without its presence?

****

At the weekly altar society meeting, Deb sat on a cold, hard, metal folding chair in the back row of the parish hall. The scent of coffee and donuts sickened her stomach. Someone at the front of the room was speaking, asking for volunteers, for what she didn't know. She couldn't focus anymore. All of her thoughts circled back to Cassidy. Since the tournament, she suspected he was drinking each and every day. He was always holed up in the master bedroom with the door closed. When he stepped into the living room to greet Adam in the afternoons, he reeked. She didn't know if the sour smell was from booze or chemotherapy.

He wouldn't let her kiss him anymore. "I'm toxic," he said, spreading his arms wide. "The doctor said no one should touch me."

He commandeered the master bathroom, cleaning up his own vomit, and washing his own clothes. Sex was out of the question. At night, he slept on the red recliner in the living room to prevent choking from the saliva draining down his throat. But during the day, he disappeared into the master bedroom. She didn't know what he did behind closed doors. Whenever she felt his presence, her stomach knotted.

"Is this seat taken?" Elliot tapped his fingers against the metal chair beside her.

Deb glanced up into his green eyes and shook her head.

The chair creaked against his weight. An elbow jostled her.

Frowning, she inched away. He was too close, as usual.

"How's your husband doing?" He leaned toward her.

A faint whiff of cologne ignited her senses. Since Cassidy's illness, he no longer smelled of woodsy shaving cream or musky deodorant. He reeked of chemicals. "Not well." She scooted her hips near the opposite edge of the seat, as far away from Elliot as possible.

"I'm sorry to hear he's not better." He crossed an ankle over a knee. "How's treatment going?"

She shrugged. "He's at the doctor's office right now." At least, she hoped he was.

"I'm praying for you, my sober saint."

With a sidelong glance, she studied him. He gazed directly at her, the eyes large and solemn. If he hadn't seduced Geraldine, then Deb might have trusted him. "Thank you." She tucked her hands underneath her armpits and focused her attention on the speaker at the front of the room.

"Do you have any help?"

"With Adam?" She tensed her shoulders. Did Elliot know what a handful that young man was? Adam woke up every night, asking for juice or a snack, and sometimes refusing to return to bed. Once he sat beside his sleeping father, rocking back and forth, until four a.m. Before her eyelids fluttered closed, she coaxed him back to his bedroom with a cookie. Exhaustion pooled in her limbs, but she refused to call Stephanie. She didn't want to let that woman know she had won. Deb would continue to persist. She would show everyone she was a competent wife and stepmother, even if the effort destroyed her. "His mother has him every weekend."

"Not enough." Elliot wagged his head. "You need a team of professionals—housekeeper, nurse, babysitter, and errand-runner—if you want to survive the next few weeks." He placed a hand on top of hers.

She expected his hot skin to scald her, but the warmth of his touch released a tremor throughout her body like a plucked guitar string. The sensation reverberated, echoing in the far reaches where no one else dared to go. She batted away his hand. "Please, don't touch me. I don't want to end up like Geraldine."

With a huff, he crumpled his fingers into a fist. "I'm not here to take advantage of you. I'm here to be a friend." When he swallowed, the Adam's apple in his throat slid up and down. "Make one mistake. Everyone remembers. Do a good deed. Everyone forgets."

He appeared as pained and miserable as she felt. "I'm sorry." She thinned her lips.

"I'll stick to prayers." Frowning, he stood. "Be well, my sober saint." He exited through the back door.

The oppressive heat breathed into the parish hall. His broad figure cut a lonely silhouette between the cars in the parking lot. After placing her hand on the vacant seat, she felt the warmth of his once-present body penetrated her skin. Sadness and loneliness descended, eclipsing suspicion and doubt. What if he only did want to help? She chased him away. How could she get him back?

Chapter Eleven

Blasting the air-conditioner in the truck, Cassidy drove past Larry's Deli. He didn't want to talk to anyone. Turning down another road, he avoided the convenience store where the clerk, a young man who should have been in college, sold him a six-pack each day without asking why he wanted beer before noon. *I can't drink*. The doctor's mandate flashed in neon lights in his mind, warning him of consequences that affected everyone around him. In the absence of something to numb the pain of his existence, he gripped the steering wheel tighter. Breathing deeper, he focused.

After parking in the driveway, he strode to the front door. Inside the living room, the heat felt worse. Turning on the ceiling fans, he sank onto the recliner. Heaviness pooled in his limbs. A fog drifted over his thoughts. He stared at the whirring blades pushing warm air around the room. He glanced at the clock. Deb would be home in an hour. A grumble rumbled through his stomach. He should eat. The sores in his mouth and throat felt like sunburns. Glancing at the silver IV pole near the window, he grimaced. *Maybe I should hook up the feeding tube*. Dragging his feet, he padded to the stuffy garage and opened one of the boxes of high-protein, plant-based formula. In the kitchen, he flushed the feeding tube with water. In the living room, he shook the formula before pouring it into the feeding container and closing the cap. He attached the syringe to the tube in his stomach, adjusted the clamp like he was shown at the hospital, and hung the feeding container on the silver IV pole. Relaxing on the recliner, he stared at the thick, white fluid flowing down into his body.

From the table beside him, his cell phone pinged several times. He grabbed the phone and swiped his finger across the screen. Three messages, one right after the other, filled his inbox. The first was from Lionel.

—*Geraldine wants to know if you'll come to the renewal of our wedding vows after the World Masters Tournament. Let me know by the end of the week. You can be my best man again.*—

Cassidy sighed. After all the heartache Geraldine caused by taking her flirting too far with another man, Lionel chose to forgive her. Sure, they attended therapy, endured countless fights, and moments of despair. For a while, after the discovery of the close encounter bordering on an affair, Lionel lived with Nick, too heartbroken and disgusted to even look at his wife. But in the end, their love prevailed. Cassidy smiled. From his experience with Deb, he knew second chance love was always sweeter. He tapped his fingers on the tiny screen.

—*Not sure. Have to ask doctor if I can skip a few days of treatment. Will let you know soon.*—

The second message was from Nick.

—*How did the doctor's appointment go?*—

Cassidy winced. Since he started drinking, he wouldn't let Nick drive him to his doctor's appointments. He didn't want anyone to know of his weakness. But with his new resolve, he needed the presence of his friend to buffer the threat of temptation. Slowly, he typed his response.

—Not good. Need to use feeding tube. Need to stay hydrated. Need to follow doctor's orders. Are you available tomorrow at two-thirty? I need a ride to chemo.—

The third message was from Stephanie.

—How are you feeling? I'm worried about you. When can I visit?—

Cassidy tensed his jaw and set aside the phone, choosing not to respond. He hadn't communicated with Stephanie since she agreed to care for Adam every weekend. Was she really worried? Or was she only concerned he might die and leave her with Adam full-time? Then what would happen to her acting career? What would happen with her freedom? She would have to relocate to Vine Valley and return to working in commercials and industrials in the city while Adam was in day care, which was her old life, minus him.

He tapped his fingers against the arms of the recliner and stared at the family photographs on the built-in bookcase against the opposite wall. Most of the pictures were of Adam at various ages, from birth to now. Above the fireplace, in a silver frame, was a picture from his second wedding. He stood in a black suit between Deb in a white wedding dress and Adam in a button- down shirt and slacks in front of the church where Deb volunteered. The photograph from his first wedding was somewhere in the attic. He didn't give it to Stephanie when she requested it in the divorce because he was angry for her wanting him to stay in an unhappy union. Sure, she was the reason for his discontent, but he could have solved the problem earlier, even before they had Adam.

Thinking back, he could have told Deb he loved her when they sat cross-legged on the floor reading poetry to each other during high school summer writing camp. But he didn't. Loyalty bound him to Stephanie. After all, she was his first girlfriend. She lived next door, welcoming him to Vine Valley the moment he arrived. When he answered her knock on his front door, he fell in love with her dazzling smile and boundless energy. Taking him under her wing, she showed him around Vine Valley, filling him in on the town's history, and introducing him to some of his lifelong friends. She loved him with a wild abandon, always putting him first. When she learned a scouting agent recommended him for the major leagues, Stephanie encouraged him to go. She would release him. She would have the child alone. But he didn't go. He couldn't leave her. He owed her and the child. So he stayed. Year after year, he remained. The happiness he experienced as a teenager slowly burned into a mirthless wonder of duty, obligation, and familial love.

No wonder the affair with Deb blindsided him. Stephanie always said he was having a typical midlife crisis. He hated her assessment of the situation. He wasn't typical. His love for Deb wasn't a crisis. Looking back, he wasn't even in midlife. Closing his eyes, he shuddered. He was at the beginning of the end.

****

When Deb returned home from the altar society meeting, she was surprised to see Cassidy in the living room, sitting on the recliner. She set her purse on the coffee table and turned up the ceiling fan as high as it would oscillate. Even then, sweat continued to coalesce along her hairline.

"How was the meeting?" Cassidy asked.

"Fine." She eyed the feeding tube streaming water into his stomach. "I'm surprised you're not in the bedroom." Perching on the edge of the sofa, she searched his face. Although his jowls sagged, he was hard and resolute. *Something happened at the doctor's office.* The premonition swarmed up her legs like a hive of bees. "How did your appointment go?"

Staring at the floor, he shrugged.

In the ensuing silence, she considered her options: nag him or leave him alone. His immobility frightened her. With a quick glance at the clock, she decided to be useful in the moments before Adam arrived home. She padded through the kitchen and descended the steps into the stuffy garage, turning on the overhead lights. In a cardboard box, she found the formula. She would stock each bag in the pantry for easy access. Bending, she lifted the first two bags. A glint of silver caught the edge of her vision. Her heartbeat hammered in her throat, and she lowered her legs. With trembling fingers, she rooted around the open mouth of a plastic garbage bag full of crushed beer cans. The stench overpowered her, and her stomach lurched. Standing, she dropped the formula, raced up the steps, and darted through the kitchen. Every nerve in her body buzzed with anger and frustration. Sliding to a stop before the recliner, she shuddered. "Why did you lie?" She balled her hands into fists. "You said you weren't drinking."

He widened his eyes and held her gaze. "I'm *not* drinking." He pointed toward the IV pole. "I'm hydrating."

With buckling knees, she crumpled to the carpet.

"There are empty beer cans in the garage." She heaved a sob. "Don't tell me those belong to Adam."

Blinking, he sighed. "I'm not drinking *anymore*."

"You never stopped, did you?" She raised her head and gulped air. "You've been drinking throughout your treatment." Shaking her head, she batted away the tears streaming down her cheeks. "No wonder you've lost weight. No wonder you have sores in your mouth. No wonder you've been hiding in our bedroom." Wheezing, she paused. The colors of the room shimmied beneath her watery gaze. Every suspicious thought haunting her consciousness these past few weeks was true. Cassidy wasn't following doctor's orders. He was drinking instead. Another thought, unbidden, rose in her mind. Lifting her head, she narrowed her gaze. "Do you *want* to die?"

He averted his gaze. "No, I don't…I'm sorry."

The pathetic weakness in his voice didn't penetrate the fortress around her heart. "I can't believe I left the convent for *you*." She waved a hand up and down the length of his body on the recliner.

Lifting his chin, he frowned. "Do you regret loving me, or do you regret leaving God?"

His question hung in the air. The buzz of the ceiling fan matched the frantic ticking of her heart. She bowed her head, her gaze drifting to a spot on the carpet. For a long moment, she thought.

Outside, a horn honked.

The bus. Adam. She rose on unsteady legs. Thoughts circled her mind like vultures looking for a fresh kill. With one sweeping glance at her husband's emaciated body, she straightened her shoulders. "I don't know." The statement hung like a tightrope between them. She balanced on the words, waiting for a response that never arrived. Turning, she opened the door and crashed into the heat, ready to retrieve her stepson. The vultures descended on her doubts. She recalled Elliot sitting beside her in the parish hall, the solemn concern in his green eyes. His wife died of cancer. Plunging a hand into her pocket, she rubbed the pads of her fingers against the rosary beads. *He knows. He understands.* Only fear of being lured into an unwanted seduction kept her from confiding in him.

The bus exhaled, and its doors folded open.

Adam staggered down the stairs. As soon as his foot touched the pavement, he clutched her outstretched arm. "Juice."

The weight of his body leaned against her, an unwanted burden. He smelled like a mixture of earth and salt from playing outside.

"Let's go inside for juice." She spoke the words in a singsong voice like she was talking to a toddler and not an adult.

"Juice." He flapped his hand, then bit a finger.

She tightened her hold on his other arm. "We're almost there." She nudged him along the walkway to the oppressive house.

He shoved his shoulder against her arm. "Juice!"

Opening the door, she steered him away from the living room and into the kitchen.

Flopping onto his chair, he slapped the table. "Juice."

She opened the refrigerator and plunged a straw into a juice box.

After seizing the box out of her hands, he sucked and gulped. The box crumpled into a concave heap of plastic in his fist. He tossed aside the wreckage and patted the table. "More." Smiling, he craned his neck. "Please."

For a long moment, she considered the request. From experience, if she gave into his demands, she would exhaust the supply of juice boxes before dinner. But if she didn't comply, she might face a wrestling match. Even though he was thinner than Cassidy, he was still a man with enough upper body strength to yank a juice box out of her hands and dart down the hallway to his room. Sighing, she grabbed another juice box from the refrigerator door and poked a straw through the aluminum seal. Only five years ago, she knelt in the cool cavern of the convent, praying to a perfect lover. Now, she cared for a thirsty, young man who spoke in monosyllables. Her stepson. From a marriage to a mortal man. A man who was drinking himself to death while cancer ravaged his insides. A knot tightened in her stomach. She collapsed into a chair next to Adam, propped her elbows on the table, and cradled her head in her hands. *I don't want this life.* She rubbed her palms over her face, fighting back tears. *Dear God, how can I escape from this mess?*

Chapter Twelve

Two weeks. Fourteen days since Cassidy stopped drinking. Fourteen days since the nausea that pitched his stomach the day after chemo didn't include the extra slosh of beer in his gut. Fourteen days after he hauled the garbage bag of smashed cans into the recycling bin. Fourteen days after the sores in his mouth started to heal. Fourteen days of listening to his wife harp, nag, and hover. She circled him relentlessly when he felt her attentions would be better spent on Adam. He was out of control—rummaging through the pantry, opening up every juice box in the fridge, tantruming with his fists and feet against the wall, and wailing and howling in the middle of the night when he should have been asleep.

"Can't you control the man?" Cassidy sat on the recliner, the feeding tube attached to the formula bag on the IV pole, for his mid-morning snack.

Deb gathered yesterday's mail off the coffee table to dust. She sprayed lemon-scented oil, covering the wood with a thin sheen. "I'm not strong like you. And I'm not his parent. He doesn't listen to me." Frowning, she wiped the surface with an old cloth, then tossed the rag in the laundry basket full of dirty clothes on the sofa. She stalked across the room and grabbed the vacuum cleaner from the hall closet.

The *vroom-vroom* sound rattled inside his head. He

couldn't talk over the noise, his voice already thin and weary. The vacuum propelled closer. He lifted his feet. Why did she have to clean every day now? Shouldn't she be at the church volunteering? Why did she hover around him until Adam arrived home? Had she stopped trusting him since she discovered he was drinking? Didn't she realize he stopped?

As soon as the noise ended, he lifted a hand, flagging for her attention. "I'm not strong anymore. I can't pick up anything over ten pounds."

She stood before him, a hand on her hip. "You're still his parent."

Sighing, he shook his head. If he wasn't hooked up, he would stand, brace his hands on her shoulders, and rattle some sense into her thick skull. "You're the adult. He's the child. You can't let him control the situation. You have to stop him from getting up in the middle of the night and raiding the kitchen."

She lifted her head and threw up her arms. "Stop comparing me to you. I parent differently."

"You don't parent at all." His voice broke into a cough. The hacking spell sliced the inside of his throat. He paused, not sure if he could continue. When caring for Adam, she did the bare minimum—changing his soiled diapers, feeding him, bathing him, and tucking him into bed with a set of prayers. She never engaged him in play or conversation. Only when he brought his music to her did she change the song. She acted more like hired help than a stepmother. After standing, he unhooked the empty formula bag from the IV pole. "You parent me more than you parent Adam."

She jabbed a finger toward his chest. "You can't be trusted."

"Is that the reason why you stopped your volunteer work?" He steered around her into the hallway.

She stepped in front of him, blocking the path to the kitchen. "When I know you're with Nick at the hospital for your treatment, I leave the house. If I stay out later, then I don't know what you're doing." She heaved a sigh. "I can't afford to have you drink yourself to death."

"How many times do I have to tell you I'm *not* drinking?" He shook the empty formula bag in her face. "I'm following doctor's orders."

She wagged her head from side to side. "I don't trust you."

With his elbow, he nudged her.

She broadened her stance and spread her arms across the width of the doorway.

"Move." A pulse twitched near his eyelid. He didn't want to hurt her, but he wanted her out of the way. He needed to clear the feeding tube and refill the formula bag with water.

Narrowing her eyes, she thrust her jaw forward. "No. I won't move until you apologize for accusing me of being a bad stepmother."

Heaving his shoulders, he considered his options. If he barreled past her, he might knock them both off balance and crash against the wall. If he slunk back into the living room, he would admit defeat. The ticking in his chest felt like a time bomb. "You're worse at parenting than Stephanie was." He pivoted into the foyer, scooped his keys out of the dish beside the front door, and stepped out into the blazing heat. After tossing the empty formula bag into the trash, he opened the door of the truck and slid inside.

Deb rushed out of the house, waving her hands overhead. "Wait! Where are you going?"

He revved the engine. The air-conditioner spat out dry heat. He adjusted the vents and snapped on the radio. A wail of drums beat all around him. Shifting the gear into Reverse, he backed out of the driveway. When he was parallel to the curb, he powered down the window and thrust his head toward his bewildered wife standing in the driveway. "Anywhere but here."

****

Without thinking, Deb dashed into the house, grabbed her purse off the end table, and locked the front door. She slid into her four-door sedan, slammed the door, and started the engine. By the time she backed out of the driveway, she was already two blocks behind Cassidy's white truck.

Sweat dripped down the sides of her face, and she switched on the air-conditioner. Steering right, she careened around a corner too closely. The back tire hitched up and over the curb. Her pulse zigzagged through her body. She gripped the steering wheel and gritted her teeth.

Cassidy's truck veered left past the convenience store.

Where was he going? She frowned, pressing a foot against the accelerator. *Why did he want to escape? Wasn't marriage supposed to be the start of happily-ever-after?* She slammed on the brakes at a red light. The tires squealed. She jerked forward then back against the sticky, leather seat. *How had the relationship disintegrated into a cat-and-mouse car chase?*

Up ahead, Cassidy sped forward, pausing only

briefly to make a left turn.

As soon as the light switched to green, Deb rammed her foot against the accelerator. The car shot forward past the speed limit. A stream of opposing traffic prevented her from swinging left to follow him. She slammed the brakes and craned her neck, searching for his vehicle.

The truck barreled down a side street and swerved right toward downtown.

By the time traffic cleared, she was already fifteen seconds behind his last turn. She circled Courthouse Square, hoping to catch his vehicle in a parking spot. No such luck. Downshifting, she slowed to a crawl to circle the perimeter one final time. Glancing left to right, she scanned the sidewalks and storefronts.

Cassidy and his truck were nowhere.

After passing by the Wapi Museum, Deb steered into a parking spot and shut off the engine. Stepping outside, she felt a wall of heat surround her like a tight embrace. She locked the car and strode past the twelve-foot high windows of the museum and tugged on the door. A swoosh of cool air pelted her face. A bell pinged, signaling her entrance.

A young Native American woman strode toward her and waved a hand around the room. "Welcome to the Wapi Museum."

Deb hadn't visited since Hope moved out of the upstairs apartment and converted the space from an art gallery into a museum. A breathtaking wood sculpture of a woman wrestling a bear caught her gaze. The sinuous curves of the woman's half-exposed breast matched the curved spine of the battling bear. Together, the two halves coalesced into a single image of human and nature. She sighed. She suddenly felt like the woman wrestling the bear, only the bear was Cassidy.

The young Native American woman took a step forward and smiled. "May I help you?"

Deb frowned, glancing at the name tag on the woman's caftan gown. "Michelle?" Was this the same woman whose secret pregnancy by her abusive boyfriend almost destroyed Lionel and Geraldine's marriage?

"Yes." Michelle widened her smile.

"I'm looking for Hope." Deb scanned the room full of bear pelts, woven baskets, and paintings of the Wapi River before the founding of Vine Valley.

"I'm sorry, but Hope is at a tribal council meeting. May I be of some assistance?"

Somewhere a baby squawked.

Michelle excused herself and wandered through the maze of artwork to a playpen by the cash register. Bending, she lifted a toddler into her arms. The little girl had a tuft of black hair, chubby cheeks, and thick legs. Michelle bounced her against her hip and cooed a Wapi lullaby.

The bell jangled against the door. "I'm sorry I'm late." Lionel strode into the gallery with a wide smile. He scooped the baby out of Michelle's arms and tossed the baby into the air. As soon as he caught her in his arms, he kissed both of her cheeks, one right after the other. "How's my goddaughter today?"

The baby giggled and patted his face.

"Hey, Deb. What brings you here?" Lionel met her gaze.

"I was looking for Hope." A pang of envy squeezed her chest. Why did Lionel look as comfortable as Cassidy in the presence of a child? What was wrong with her? Didn't she have a maternal bone in her body? She batted away the thoughts and tightened her smile. "How's Geraldine?"

"Anxious as a first-time bride." He chuckled. "She's spending too much time picking out a dress for the renewal of our vows. I don't know why she won't wear her old dress."

Michelle wagged a finger. "A woman never wears the same dress twice."

"Only if she's a little princess." Lionel rubbed the stubble on his chin against the baby's cheek until she erupted in laughter. "Am I right, Leilani?"

Giggling, Leilani cupped his face with her small hands.

"She loves you." The words slipped out of Deb's mouth. "I wish Adam would love me."

Lionel strapped Leilani into a baby carrier and grabbed a diaper bag. "He does. He just can't show it like everyone else because he's autistic."

Michelle held open the door and leaned over to kiss her daughter's cheek. "See you tonight, sweetheart." She touched Lionel's arm. "Thank you for watching her."

"I should be thanking you." Lionel grinned and nodded. "See you both later."

As soon as the bells tinkled again, Deb cast down her head. Why was she trying so hard? A knot tightened in her stomach. Why was she chasing her husband? A pulse of worry throbbed in her temples. Why had she let her life go from bad to worse?

Chapter Thirteen

After checking the rearview mirror one last time, Cassidy parked in the back lot of Jasper's Bar and Grill. With a quiver in his step, he crunched over the gravel to the side entrance and took a seat at the bar beneath an air-conditioning vent. When the bartender asked him what he would like to drink, he ordered a beer. *Just one.* He deserved some refreshment after winning the high-speed chase through town. The foamy pint tasted crisp and bitter. As always, when he swallowed, he winced. Warm relief spread throughout his body. Among the cold beer, the colored glass bottles in the mirror behind the bar, and the light air-conditioning, he felt free for the first time in two weeks.

The phone in his pocket buzzed. He swiped the screen and squinted at the message.

—Where are you? When are you coming home?—

He set aside the phone and glanced around the room at the other patrons. A few college kids sat in booths, drinking beers and eating hamburgers and fries. An elderly man hunched at the other end of the bar, sipping a drink through a straw and reading a paperback novel. The bartender washed and dried glasses while watching sports highlights on the bank of TVs above the bar.

When the bells chimed against the glass doors, he glanced over his shoulder and witnessed his ex-wife sashay into the room. *Beautiful and crazy*. The phrase he called Stephanie all those years they were married because of her drop-dead gorgeous curves and anything-goes-attitude in the bedroom. Even now, she was slim and attractive. Seeing her at this moment, he no longer felt a zing of energy and hopefulness. Now he only felt the lingering dread over how things ended.

The bartender glanced over and smiled. "Hey, Hollywood. You're early today."

"I just got my nails done."

The sound of her heels *clip-clopping* on the hardwood floor echoed against the wood-paneled walls.

Smiling, she wiggled her red talons and climbed on the barstool next to Cassidy. "I'll have a diet soda and a garden salad, no dressing." Tapping her nails on the counter, she frowned at the empty pint. "Still drinking?"

He tipped the almost-empty glass and stared at the foam. "Believe it or not, I quit for two weeks."

"Why'd you start again?" She thanked the bartender for the drink and sipped the diet soda.

His phone pinged with another text. He swiped the screen.

—You better not be drinking and driving. I'll call 9-1-1 and report your license plate.—

The hairs on the back of his neck bristled. How dare she assume the worst? Sure, he was drinking. But he wasn't driving. He slid the phone toward Stephanie and pointed toward the messages. "Go ahead and scroll, then you'll know why I'm drinking." He swallowed the last of the beer and slammed the glass against the counter.

She flicked a manicured finger up the screen.

"Deb's not a hysterical woman. She wouldn't accuse you of something you didn't do."

"I drove here sober." His resolve to drink only one beer melted beneath the heat of his anger. "But I'm tempted to get drunk."

"Don't." She waved for the bartender. "A glass of water for the gentleman."

"Right away, Hollywood." The bartender winked and set a glass of iced water on the counter.

Remembering how she always parented him like she parented Adam, he narrowed his gaze. He shifted on the bar stool and squared his shoulders. "What if I want another beer?"

"Don't." She motioned toward the bartender. "No more booze for the gentleman."

Cassidy scoffed. "You can't control me. You aren't married to me anymore."

"But she is." Stephanie tapped a finger on the phone. "She's threatening to call 911 and report you for drinking and driving."

"She won't." He snatched the phone out of her hand. A trickle of dread leaked through his pores. Would she?

"Don't tempt her." She nodded toward the glass. "Drink your water. And tell her where you are and when you'll be home."

He set the phone on the counter. "I thought you guys hated each other."

She shrugged. "I was the wife once. I know how she feels." She thanked the bartender for the salad and stabbed her fork into a slice of tomato.

"Wait." He lifted a hand to grab the bartender's attention. "Don't listen to Miss Hollywood here. I'm paying my own tab, and I'll have another beer."

Frowning, she pointed toward the bartender. "No beer." Pursing her lips, she nodded toward Cassidy. "Answer your wife."

"Why are you nagging me?" He thrust back his shoulders. "We aren't married anymore."

"I would keep my mouth shut if you knew how to take care of yourself." She glowered at the phone. "Please don't keep her waiting. I would have dialed 911 by now."

A moment of hesitation filled him. *Was his drinking that big of a problem?* He clenched his jaw, remembering how his mother followed him during high school to stop him from sneaking drinks at the convenience store with friends, leaving him no choice but to fill his thermos with beer. Stephanie removed the cold ones he hid in the ice chest he packed for work each day, forcing him to stop by the liquor store each night instead. He crumpled his hand into a fist. Now Deb pursued him in a wild car chase through downtown to make sure he wasn't drinking. *Why do I keep surrounding myself with the same type of woman?* For a long moment, he stared at his phone. *Unless.* He pursed his lips. *I am the problem.*

****

On the other side of town, safe in the confines of her home, Deb paced the length of the living room from the picture window overlooking the front yard to the threshold where a crucifix hung from the wall. *Jesus, Mary, Joseph, pray for us*. After losing Cassidy in the car chase, she drove home. When praying the rosary didn't ease her restless legs or worrisome thoughts, she stood and paced. Glancing out the window, she wondered. *Where is he?* No traffic on the quiet cul-de-sac. *Why isn't he responding to my texts?* She glared at the phone in her hand, willing it to ring. A moment later, as if answering her prayers, a vibration jiggled her palm, and a light flashed. With her pulse thrumming in her throat, she swiped the screen and read the text from Cassidy.

—*Don't call 911. I'm at Jasper's. Be home soon.*—

Gaping at the words, she fumed. *Why is he drinking at Jasper's?* She paused. Elliot must not be working. He would never serve him beer, knowing about his cancer diagnosis. *Should I call 911 anyway?* The bitter taste of bile filled her mouth. Scrolling through her contacts, she found Cassidy's number. She waited for two rings before he answered.

"Hey, Deb."

He sounded coy and shaken, his voice thin and watery.

Blood thumped in her temples. She gripped the phone tighter. "You know we don't patronize Jasper's." After Geraldine's romantic encounter with Elliot, she, Hope, and Geraldine decided to relocate ladies' night out to another location.

"I know. I'm sorry. I'm on my way home."

He sounded sober, the words clear and precise, but she had to know for sure. "Have you been drinking?" She scrunched her shoulders toward her ears, listening for his response.

"One beer. I promise."

Anger flooded her body. As she clenched the phone tighter, her hand shook. How dare he risk his chemo treatments! One beer was one too many. *Calm down.* She breathed in deeply and held the air in her lungs. Exhaling, she closed her eyes for a moment. *What to do?* If she ranted about the illicit drink, she suspected he might get upset, decide to stay, and have another to spite her. Opening her eyes, she nudged back her shoulders and assumed a tone of confidence. "Thank you for telling me the truth. I look forward to seeing you soon."

"Love you."

A tentative relief snaked across her shoulders, and she loosened her grip on the phone. "I love you, too."

Outside, a horn honked.

She glanced out the window and noticed the bus parked in the driveway. "I've got to go. Adam's home." After ending the call, she strode out of the house, blinking in the hot afternoon sunlight. She skirted around the lawn and stood on the pavement.

The bus driver folded the doors. "He's had a bad day."

Haven't we all? Deb punched her fists against her waist and waited. *One problem after another.*

Adam bit his fingers and stomped his feet at the top of the stairs.

Don't react. A behavior specialist said any negative response would magnify Adam's unwanted actions by a thousand. With calm reserve, she inhaled and counted. *One, two, three…* When she counted to ten, she opened her arms and forced a smile. "Come here, Adam. Let's go inside for some juice."

Shaking his head, he howled.

"Looks like you'll have to get him, ma'am."

I'm not strong enough. When angry, Adam could lift twice his weight and slam it against the wall. In a handful of years, he'd broken three TVs and two chairs.

"One moment…" She dashed into the cool house, retrieved his computer tablet full of music, and seized a box of cookies from the pantry. Darting across the pathway, she lifted each arm. "Want music? Want a cookie?"

He widened his eyes and grabbed the handrail. "Cookie." He took a step downward.

Deb placed the computer tablet by her feet, ripped open the box, and removed a chocolate chip cookie. The rich, sweet scent lingered on her fingertips even after Adam swiped it.

"More." He chewed with his mouth open, drool oozing from the corners of his lips.

"Go inside for more." She nudged him forward before stooping to retrieve the computer tablet.

"I want more!" He lunged for the box, tearing it from her hand. Within moments, he shoved a handful of cookies into his mouth. The box tumbled from his fingers, and the remaining cookies scattered onto the lawn. He fell to his knees and scooped up the cookies along with handfuls of grass, stuffing whatever he could between his lips.

"No, don't." Deb dropped the computer tablet and gathered as many cookies into her hands as she could.

"More." He batted her arm.

Wincing from the sharp slaps, she withdrew.

"I want more." He staggered with flailing arms.

I wish Cassidy was here. He would know how to handle a bad tantrum better than me. Turning, she ran to the side of the house and dumped the dirty cookies into the foul-smelling trash can.

Adam hit her back with his open palms. "More."

Pain slapped through her. She spun, arms shielding

her face and elbows knocking against him.

He stumbled back a few steps and hollered. "More." Jumping up and down, he bit his fingers.

Gasping, Deb rushed back to the lawn and grabbed the computer tablet. Swiping the screen, she tapped Play on Adam's favorite song. The chords floated up like invisible bubbles bursting on the warm air.

The first rush of instrumentals powered through his tantrum. He dropped his fingers from his mouth and panted.

Like the Piped Piper, Deb lured Adam into the house and shut the door. "Go to your room." She handed him the computer tablet and pointed toward the hallway. As soon as the bedroom door clicked shut, she collapsed on the sofa, every muscle in her body sore. *I did it*. A flush of pride swelled beneath the pain. *I'm not such a bad stepmom, after all*. She closed her eyes and gulped a few breaths. Who cared if she lost a box of cookies or suffered a few bruises from the battle? The fight with Adam was over, even if the war with Cassidy had just begun.

Chapter Fourteen

After finishing the glass of water, Cassidy slipped off the barstool and wavered for a moment. The lights in the room spun, and he gripped Stephanie's arm.

"Are you okay?" She furrowed her brow, tucking her wallet into her purse.

He breathed in deeply and studied the lights above the bar, which had stilled into clarity. "Yeah, I think so." He nodded, releasing her arm.

Squinting, she peered closer. "You look a little pallid. Did you have chemo today?"

Shaking his head, he swallowed and winced. "Yesterday." Since he stopped working, he found it hard to keep track of the days. He clutched his stomach, which felt like twisted ropes. "I've started using the feeding tube. My mouth hurts too much to eat."

Stephanie patted the space beside her. "Why don't you sit a moment? I'll pull my car to the front of the restaurant and drive you home."

A jolt of panic ripped through him. He imagined a confrontation—Deb running out of the house and pummeling Stephanie with insults the moment she steered into the driveway, and Stephanie's cool rebuttal emphasizing Deb's lack of control over the whole situation. Pain squeezed his chest. "No, I'll be fine." Grabbing the edge of the counter, he steadied his legs.

The lines beside her mouth deepened. "You don't

look fine."

Nausea settled in the bottom of his stomach, but fatigue traveled up his legs. He forced a smile. "I appreciate your concern, but I don't need any help." Slowly, he swiveled. He let go of the counter and stepped away. The floor tilted. The ceiling crashed down. The colors of the room spun and dissolved into a rainbow of confusion. He lost his balance and toppled into a heap on the hardwood floor.

"Cass, are you all right?" Stephanie knelt before him and shouted at the bartender. "Call an ambulance."

Her face wavered in zigzagged lines, fading in and out. "I'm fine." The words floated from his mouth like soap bubbles, bursting one right after the other. Slowly, his vision narrowed until Stephanie's concerned face became a pinpoint of light, and the rest of the world darkened.

****

"Where's Cassidy?" Deb eyed the clock on the stove. Six-thirty. Over the past three and a half hours, she repeatedly called his phone, each time reaching voice mail until the mailbox was full and could no longer receive any messages. Finally, she called Jasper's Bar and Grill, but the bartender on duty asked around and said no one had seen Cassidy Burke. Maybe he could call the bartender before him and see if he knew anything. Thirty minutes passed without a return call. Maybe the bartender was swallowed up by happy hour.

She lifted the lid to the pot of bubbling spaghetti sauce. Fresh rosemary and basil from the backyard garden wafted in a cloud of steam. Through the kitchen window, the sun started to set below the fence. A stream of golden light flooded the warm, cozy kitchen.

Adam wandered into the room. A screaming guitar solo ripped into the silence. He thrust the computer tablet against her side. "Song." He covered an ear with one hand and frowned.

Sighing, Deb wiped her hands on a dish towel and swiped the screen. After scrolling through the options, she settled on a quiet melody. Tinkling notes from a piano tumbled into the room.

"Thank you." Smiling, Adam snatched the computer tablet and loped away.

Just as the melody receded, Deb's cell phone rang from the kitchen counter.

After turning down the burner on the stove, she covered the pot of spaghetti sauce and squinted at the caller ID. A jolt of surprise rocketed through her body. *Why is Stephanie calling?* Frustration tightened her spine. She turned over the phone, ignoring the intrusion. *I don't have anything to say to that woman. She's probably angry because she wants to talk to Cassidy and his mailbox is full.*

She set the table with three spaces for her, Adam, and Cassidy. Waiting for the water to boil for the noodles, she paced the length of the kitchen.

Again, the phone rang.

She flipped over the phone on the counter and peered at the caller ID. Stephanie again. A bristle of annoyance tightened her jaw. That woman was persistent. She even left a message. Frowning, Deb turned away from the call and dumped the noodles into the boiling water.

A couple of minutes later, her phone rang again. An unknown number flashed on the screen. A spike of adrenaline raced through her blood. Who was calling? She hesitated a moment. Was Stephanie spoofing her number to get through? Shaking her head at the ridiculous thought, she swiped a finger across the screen. "Hello?"

"Mrs. Burke?"

A man's voice tunneled through the line. Not Stephanie. She released her breath and relaxed her shoulders. "Speaking."

"I'm Ted, a nurse, from Vine Valley Hospital. Your husband, Cassidy Burke, has been admitted."

Admitted? Her breath tangled in her throat. "But-but—" She stumbled over her words. A prickle of fear zinged up her spine. Images of car crashes flashed through her mind. She clutched a fist against the ache in her chest. "Was he drinking and driving?"

"No, ma'am. He collapsed from low blood pressure. We're keeping him for observation."

Collapsed. Observation. She grabbed the nearest chair and sat, her thoughts traveling back to her mother's sickness. The same situation at the same hospital with the same result. She sobbed. *No, God, please not again.* She gripped the phone tighter. "How long will he be there?"

"At least forty-eight hours."

She gasped. She would be stuck all alone with Adam unless she called Stephanie. Was Stephanie calling to relieve her of Adam's care? If so, how did Stephanie know? Did the hospital contact her first? A flicker of frustration fanned in her belly. Had Cassidy forgotten to update his emergency contact list? "When can I see him?"

"Visiting hours end at eight."

"Thank you." She jabbed her finger on the red button and glanced at the clock on the stove. One hour. She curled a hand into a fist and held it against her temples. Who could watch Adam for one hour? She scrolled through her list of contacts and dialed Geraldine.

"Hey, sugar. What's up?"

The sweet, singsong voice of her friend buoyed her spirits. "I need help. Cassidy was admitted to the hospital. I need someone to watch Adam for the next hour, so I can visit him. Are you available?"

"Oh, goodness, no. I'm so sorry," Geraldine gasped. "I'd love to help, but I'm busy catering a dinner tonight. Have to get business wherever I can until the store opens."

"I understand." Deb slumped forward and dialed Hope.

On the fourth ring, Hope answered. "Hi, Deb. May I call you back?"

"No, I have an emergency." She stood and paced. "Cassidy's in the hospital. Can you watch Adam for an hour?"

"I'd love to, but I'm heading into a tribal council meeting. Have you tried Geraldine?"

"Yes, she's catering."

"How about Stephanie?"

She flinched, widening her eyes. "No, I don't want to talk to that woman."

"She's Adam's mom. Call her." Hope sighed. "I have to go. I'll send a prayer to the Great Spirit."

"Thanks."

Adam staggered into the room and thrust the silent computer tablet against her ribs. "Song."

She placed her phone on the counter, then grabbed the tablet. She swiped the screen and poked a finger at the list of music. A cacophony of drums rattled against the windows. She handed Adam the computer tablet.

He hugged the booming music to his chest and darted from the room, leaving her alone.

She turned off the stove, drained the spaghetti, and set the pot on the table. All of her movements felt like sleepwalking. She ladled tangy-smelling sauce over slippery noodles. With a fork and knife, she cut up Adam's food into bite-sized pieces. Every action felt empty and hollow. The silence throbbed with loneliness. She strode over to the cupboard for a glass and filled it with water from the sink. On the counter, the blue light blinked on her phone. She took a sip of the lukewarm, tasteless drink. When she thought of calling back Stephanie or, at least, listening to the message, a flash of pain ached in her jaw. Scowling at the flashing light, she set the glass on the counter and turned over the phone. Pride and resentment competed for her attention, preventing her from focusing on the real problem—admitting she needed help from Stephanie.

Chapter Fifteen

Cassidy bobbed to the surface of consciousness. The fingers stroking his right hand felt small and cool. "Deb?" He blinked and opened his eyes.

"No, I'm Stephanie." She squeezed his fingers.

Focusing on her green eyes, he struggled to remember what happened. But the only things he could recall were the spinning room at Jasper's and Stephanie's voice calling for an ambulance. As he shifted his gaze, the images of the room emerged. Machines beeped, and lights glowed. An IV was hooked in the wrist that dangled by his side, as limp as a withered leaf. A hospital bracelet encircled the wrist of the hand Stephanie held. "How long have I been in the hospital?"

Stephanie twisted her lips and glanced at the clock against the wall. "Four hours."

Four hours. Worried about his wife, he cringed. "Has anyone told Deb where I am?"

"I called a couple of times, but she didn't answer." Stephanie dropped his hand and stepped back. "I left a message about fifteen minutes ago."

He attempted to lift his head from the pillow, but a jolt of pain shot from the base of his skull, jangled down his neck, and across his shoulders. Wincing, he lay back and stared helplessly at his ex-wife. Worry knotted his stomach. "She won't pick up if you call.

She hates you."

"No kidding." Frowning, she tossed back her hair. "I asked someone from the nurses' station to call her."

He glanced at the exit. *I need to see Deb.* Beside him, the machine bleeped with a spike in his blood pressure. "She can't come here anyway. She has Adam. He won't get out of the car, and she won't leave him alone." He scowled at the IV drip. Each clear droplet pooled in the space between the clear plastic bag and the tube running into the vein. He glanced around the tiny, white room. A dull ache throbbed in his chest.

Tapping her chin with a finger, Stephanie glanced up at the ceiling. "I can drive over to the house and watch Adam while Deb comes to visit."

Relief flooded his body. Stephanie was always full of solutions. She stood confident and poised beside the bed, a professional actress who knew the power of persuasion. He admired this woman who took charge of a situation with solid judgment. Why did he ever leave her? "Sounds good. I just hope she opens the door."

"She won't have a choice." Stephanie slung her purse over a shoulder and spun on her heels, *clip-clopping* out of the room.

Alone, he scratched the skin above the IV. On the TV bolted to the wall, a mirage of nature images flickered across the screen. The blinds were drawn on the window beside him. No flowers graced the bedside table. Searching, he could not find a remote for the TV. The sterility and hopelessness of his surroundings settled like a weight against the length of his body. For a long moment, he stared at the closed door with only one thought circling his mind. *I want to go home.*

****

The relentless knocking on the front door jostled Deb out of her battle with Adam to take a bath. She released his hands, letting him bolt down the hallway and slam the door to his room. Turning, she stalked through the foyer and peered out the peephole.

A red-haired woman stood beneath the glowing porch light.

Deb gulped. *Stephanie*. What was she doing here? After feeding Adam dinner and cleaning up the kitchen, Deb never bothered to listen to the voicemail or call her back. If she refused to answer the door, would Stephanie eventually leave?

"I know you're home," Stephanie shouted. "Your car's in the driveway." She pounded a fist against the door. "Please, open up. I'm here to take care of Adam, so you can see Cassidy in the hospital before visiting hours are over."

Deb stiffened her back. How did Stephanie know Cassidy was in the hospital? The phone in her back pocket rang, and she jumped. The caller ID read *Stephanie Burke*.

"Open up. I know you're there. I can hear your phone ringing."

Feeling like a child caught with a hand in the cookie jar, Deb silenced the phone and unlocked the front door.

"Finally." Frowning, Stephanie shoved her way into the foyer. "Listen. I know we aren't exactly friends, but we have two people we care about in common—Adam and Cassidy. Let's try to be civil, okay?" She jabbed a finger toward Deb's pocket. "Answer your phone the next time I call."

Anger flared in Deb's chest. *How dare she treat me*

like a child? Narrowing her gaze, she crossed her arms over her chest. "Who told you Cassidy was in the hospital?"

"No one told me." Stephanie jabbed a finger toward her chest. "I watched him pass out at Jasper's." She splayed her hands. "I was having a late lunch. He was finishing a beer. I told him to drink water and tell you where he was and what time he'd be home." She widened her eyes. "We were getting ready to leave. He collapsed." Her voice broke, and she inhaled sharply. "I rode behind the ambulance and made sure he was taken care of before I called you."

Shock paralyzed Deb's body. Was God punishing her again by letting her be the last one to know about Cassidy's current situation?

"Get your purse and go." Stephanie tapped the watch against her wrist. "You only have fifteen minutes."

Deb shook her head. How could she leave Stephanie alone in her home with Adam? What if she snooped around? "I won't let you stay in my home."

"Fine." Stephanie snarled. "Then I'll take Adam with me." She jostled past Deb. "Don't bother packing. I bought Adam clothes and a computer tablet." She tossed a hand into the air.

The *clip-clop* of her heels on the hardwood floor sounded like gunshots.

"Adam! Mommy's here! Let's go for a ride."

Quivering, Deb grabbed her purse and keys and followed them both out of the house. After locking the front door, she darted to her old, four-door sedan, started the engine, and sputtered out of the driveway. In the rearview mirror, she glimpsed Stephanie loading

Adam into Johnny's black pickup truck against the last light of the summer sun.

Five minutes later, she swerved into the hospital parking lot and found a spot close to the entrance. After grabbing her purse and locking the car door, she dashed into the warm, wide entrance.

The attendant glanced up. "May I help you?"

She gripped the counter. "I'm here to see Cassidy Burke."

The attendant typed the name into the computer. "Third floor, room 323. You'd better hurry. Visiting hours end in seven minutes."

Nodding her thanks, she bolted up the staircase, taking the steps two at a time. On the third floor, she jogged along the corridor, dodging nurses, doctors, and patients dressed in hospital gowns. Her ragged breathing pumped through her body, propelling her forward. Panting, she nudged open the door to room 323. Her husband lay in a white hospital bed with his gaze transfixed by the flickering images on the TV. Worry deflated from her chest. She softened her jaw and relaxed her shoulders. "Hey, Cass. I'm here."

He glanced over, and a slow smile spread across his face.

She tiptoed into the room and dropped her purse on the table by the window. After glancing at the IV dripping into his vein and the jagged line of the monitor tracking his heart rate, she grabbed his warm, calloused hand and curled her fingers. "How are you doing?"

"Better now you're here." He tugged her closer. "You drive faster than I thought."

"Not fast enough to catch you." She winked.

He chuckled.

After dipping her head to his face, she kissed his cheek. He smelled of sour milk and ammonia. "Stephanie took Adam." She raised her head and glanced at the clock. "I'll stay until someone kicks me out." She widened her smile and squeezed his hand.

"I'm glad Stephanie could be of help." He kept his gaze focused on her face and smiled.

He appeared so delighted to see her. The light in his hazel eyes sparkled. The freckles danced across the bridge of his nose. Her happiness was marred by a twinge of guilt over how she treated Stephanie, ignoring her phone calls and refusing to answer the front door. She dropped her gaze. Why was she so cruel to his ex-wife?

"What's wrong?" Cassidy asked.

"I wasn't kind to Stephanie." She bit her lower lip. "I didn't pick up the phone or answer the door."

Cassidy laughed. "I didn't think you would." He shook her arm. "Don't worry about what can't be changed, okay? Next time, just let her help. That's why she's here."

"Okay." Deb met his gaze and nodded.

Cassidy squinted. "What else is wrong?"

A lump formed in her throat. "I don't want to lose you to cancer like I lost my mom."

"You won't." He held her gaze and sighed. "I've decided to stop drinking for good. I'll ask Dr. Rodriguez for a referral to an outpatient treatment program."

"You will?" She raised her eyebrows and searched her husband's face. Love shone in his hazel eyes. Gratitude lightened the pain in her chest.

"I don't like disappointing you." He frowned. "And

I don't like being here. I want to be home with my family where I belong."

She nodded, although a part of her wondered how long his promise to stay sober would last.

Chapter Sixteen

Before being released from his two-day hospital stay, Cassidy asked to see Dr. Rodriguez.

She strode into room 323, swinging a clipboard, and frowned. "Mr. Burke, I wasn't expecting to see you today."

"I know. I asked to see you for a referral." He reclined in the hospital bed with his wrist taped where the IV had been. The heart monitor was no longer strapped to his chest.

She stood beside the bed and tapped a pen against the clipboard. "A referral for?"

"Outpatient treatment." He swallowed and winced. "For alcoholism."

Nodding, she scribbled something on the clipboard. She tore off the sheet and placed it in his palm. "Here's the number. I'll let the director know to expect your call."

He stared at the name and phone number of the facility: *Path to Hope Recovery Center*. A knot tightened in his stomach. "Thank you."

Smiling, she touched his shoulder. "I'm proud of you for finally taking responsibility for your health."

He nudged away, feeling fire ignite in his cheeks. He didn't like admitting anything was wrong, but the past forty-eight hours gave him a glimpse of what his life would look like without the presence of the people he loved most. He could hardly wait until he could drive over to Stephanie's place and pick up Adam before coming home.

"Good luck." She smiled before turning and walking out the door.

Alone, he flipped over the paper in his hands the same way he witnessed his wife caress her rosary beads with hope.

****

Without Cassidy or Adam being home, Deb invited her girlfriends over for an afternoon visit. Sitting in the backyard beneath the patio umbrella, she nudged the sunglasses up the bridge of her nose and waited for Hope to serve the Native American iced tea she brought.

"Nice weather, right?" Hope handed her a tall glass smelling of oranges and hibiscus.

The sun slanted through the branches of the oak tree, casting dappled shadows on the lawn. She clutched the ice-cold glass in her hands and took a tentative sip. The sweet brew melted against her tongue. "Yes. Quite lovely. Not too hot."

Geraldine sat beside her, flipping through a bridal magazine. "What do you gals think of this dress?" She slid the glossy pages across the table and pointed toward the gown in question.

Squinting, Hope frowned. "A little decadent for my tastes. What do you think, Deb?"

Deb glanced at the model wearing a tight, heart-shaped bodice of tiny rhinestones transitioning into a floor-length gown of sheer white tulle and lace. She recalled her wedding dress—a simple, white satin sheath. "I agree with Hope. That dress is too much for a second wedding."

Geraldine snatched the magazine off the table, her face flushed. "Not a second wedding, but a renewal of our wedding vows."

Hope lifted her eyebrows. "Why don't you wear your original wedding dress?"

Tossing back her head, Geraldine scoffed. "That old thing isn't stylish anymore."

"But the symbolism is priceless." Hope lifted her glass of iced tea. "I would wear the same dress if I was renewing my vows to Nick."

After laughing, Geraldine smiled. "Sugar, you wear the same dress *every* day."

Deb pinched together her lips. How could her best friend jabber on and on about some ridiculously overpriced ceremony in Las Vegas? She waved a hand toward the magazine. "Why ask us what we think if you don't value our opinions?" She huffed. "Do what you like with your special day." She crossed her arms and laid them on the wooden picnic table. "Cassidy and I probably won't be there anyway. He's still in the hospital."

Deb's outburst doused Geraldine's enthusiasm. She closed the magazine and tucked it into her purse.

"Nick said Cassidy was being released today." Hope glanced from Geraldine to Deb. "The doctor wouldn't release him unless he was better, right?"

Silently, Deb shrugged.

"Sugar, even if Cassidy has to stay, you should come to Vegas." Geraldine touched her elbow. "*You* need a break."

"How can I leave?" Deb flung open her arms. She didn't want to give Adam to Stephanie and leave

Cassidy alone. "I have to consider my family."

"Stephanie's doing a mighty fine job taking care of her son." Geraldine picked up her glass of iced tea. She gulped a few swallows, then waved her glass in the air. "I'm sure she'll keep him for as long as you'd like."

Deb didn't have the heart to tell her Cassidy was picking up Adam on his way home because he missed his son as much as he missed her. Sighing, she glanced from Geraldine to Hope. "Are you attending the ceremony?"

"I don't know." Hope bowed her head. "Lately, my attention has been directed toward the tribe. Charlene is ill. Mike's not sure if the tribe is ready for a new chief. My job is to ask the Great Spirit for guidance." She clutched her beaded necklace. "I have a vision quest scheduled the week before the World Masters. If the Great Spirit guides me to act on behalf of the tribe, I'll need to stay and help with the special election."

Geraldine pouted. "What good is renewing my vows in Vegas if my two best friends won't be there?"

"If the Great Spirit allows, I'll be there." Hope stretched an arm across the table and squeezed Geraldine's hand. "I'd love to see you and Lionel all lovey-dovey again."

"What about you, sugar?" Geraldine nudged Deb's shoulder. "Think you can give up Adam for a few days?"

"What about Cassidy?" Deb faltered, wondering if he would return to drinking without someone watching over him.

Geraldine flicked a wrist. "He'll be fine, sugar."

"Maybe you can have someone from the hospital stop by and visit," Hope suggested. "Don't they have volunteers?"

Geraldine chuckled. "I don't know if candy stripers make home visits, sugar."

"Maybe Michelle can visit." Hope lifted her shoulders. "Just to check in and see if he needs anything."

Deb wrapped her arms across her chest. "I'll think about it." She squeezed tightly, holding herself together lest she fall apart.

Chapter Seventeen

A blast of gardenias assaulted Cassidy's senses in the reception area of Path to Hope Recovery Center. The white blossoms sprouted from several vases surrounding the U-shaped table where a young woman greeted him.

"Dr. Chang will be with you shortly." She slid an intake questionnaire on a clipboard with a pen and pointed toward the bank of chairs in the lobby. "Have a seat and complete this paperwork."

He took a seat near the long, white coffee table and crossed an ankle over his leg. Squinting, he read through each question with the pen poised above the clipboard.

—Do friends, family members, or co-workers comment on your drinking?

Should he check yes or no? Only Deb and Stephanie complained. No one else cared. He decided to skip to the next question.

—Do you struggle to remember what happened when you were drinking?

What an easy question. He checked the box marked *No*. Smiling, he read the next question.

—Does your drinking cause problems at work, school, or home?

Again, he paused. The tip of the ballpoint pen hovered over the box marked *Yes*. If he hadn't ended up in the hospital last week, he could have answered *No*. Sighing, he checked the box marked *Yes* and proceeded to the next question.

—*Do you ever feel guilty about drinking?*

He recalled the forty-eight hours he spent in the hospital. Sure, guilt nagged every once in a while. But that guilt only started recently with Deb's complaints. He marked the *Yes* box and read the next question.

—*Do you ever hide your drinking?*

Heat flamed his face. *Oh, boy*. He rubbed his chin and checked the *Yes* box.

—*Have you ever been unsuccessful in stopping your alcohol consumption?*

Without further thought, he checked the *No* box. After all, he abstained for two weeks.

—*Do you think about drinking even when you aren't drinking?*

He checked the *No* box. Why think about drinking when you could just have a drink?

—*Do you feel better when you are drinking?*

Of course, he did. He checked the *Yes* box. Didn't everyone?

—*Do you ever feel worse after drinking?*

He grumbled. *That question should come with a qualifier—only after I started treatment for cancer.* Before cancer, he always felt good, no matter how much he drank. He skipped the question.

—*Do you drink to celebrate victories or forget defeats?*

Yes he checked. Who didn't?

—*Do you only drink with others?*

Easy *No* checked.

—*Do you only drink alone?*

He grinned, recalling the rounds of beer Lionel purchased for the team whenever he struck out. *No* again.

—Do you think you have a drinking problem?

With a flourish, he checked the *Yes* box. Why else would he be here? Only two more questions.

—Who referred you?

Nodding, he wrote in *Dr. Rodriguez.*

—What do you hope to accomplish after twelve weeks in our program?

Another twelve weeks? He frowned. Twelve weeks of chemo and radiation. Twelve weeks of addiction counseling. Why was everything twelve weeks? He tapped the end of the pen against the clipboard and thought of an appropriate response. Emptiness surfaced. Finally, he scribbled, *I don't know.*

"Mr. Burke?" A small man dressed in a white lab coat stood in front of the reception area.

"Over here." Cassidy stood and strolled over to the man.

"Dr. Chang." The man smiled, and ruddy apple cheeks squeezed his brown eyes almost shut. He curled his long, slender fingers over Cassidy's hand and pumped his arm in a firm handshake. "Come this way." He led him down a broad hallway and into a conference room. Pointing to the folding chairs arranged in a half circle around a white board and podium, Dr. Chang nodded. "Have a seat. We start group therapy in ten minutes."

"Group therapy?" Cassidy glanced around the room that smelled of burnt coffee and stale donuts, counting the chairs. Twelve. He would be surrounded by eleven strangers for the next hour. "I thought this rehab program was individual counseling."

Dr. Chang stood before the podium and read through the answers on the clipboard Cassidy had given him. "So, why did you leave two questions blank?"

"Which ones?" Cassidy shoved his hands into his pockets and rocked back on his heels.

Dr. Chang squinted at the clipboard. "Do friends, family, or co-workers comment on your drinking?"

"Depends. My friends are all drinkers. Like me. So are my co-workers. I often bring a couple of six-packs to the job site at the end of the week to kick off the weekend." He glanced down at the floor. "But my wife and my ex-wife aren't big drinkers. So, yeah, they make comments every now and then."

"What kind of comments?" Dr. Chang lifted his small, dark head and waited.

Cassidy shrugged. "I don't know. Just the normal comments a nagging woman makes."

Dr. Chang chuckled. "I see. My wife doesn't make those comments. I do."

"You're the nagger?" Cassidy widened his eyes, wondering what type of treatment program he just entered. Twelve weeks of Dr. Chang nagging didn't sound productive or fun.

Tapping the clipboard, Dr. Chang read off the other question. "Do you ever feel worse after drinking?"

"Only after I started treatment for cancer. Before, I felt just fine. I've been drinking since high school when my friends and I would sneak beers on the weekends. College frat parties mellowed out to social gatherings with family and friends. Now I mostly drink with my softball buddies or my construction crew."

"Until recently, yes?" Dr. Chang set aside the

clipboard. "Dr. Rodriguez thinks your throat cancer might be related to your alcohol consumption. I agree. You need to stop drinking completely."

"I know. I will. I went fourteen days without a beer. Then I got into a fight with my wife and had a cold one at a bar." Cassidy hunched his shoulders. "I don't mind stopping through treatment, but I don't know if I can make this habit a lifestyle, okay?"

Dr. Chang arched an eyebrow. "You can't stop drinking just during your cancer treatment." He pointed toward the clipboard. "You have to stop forever."

Forever? Cassidy couldn't image a life without beer. What would he tell the guys in the dugout? What would he drink during weekends and holidays? What would he tell his friends when they asked him to hang out at the local bar? What would he tell his crew at the end of a work week? He crossed his arms over his chest and broadened his stance. "Why?"

"Because the cancer will return." Dr. Chang folded his hands on the podium and straightened his lips into a firm line. "Next time, you won't be lucky. You might die."

"I could die this time." Cassidy threw open his arms and gazed at the ceiling. "I'm not done with treatment yet. I have a few more weeks to go."

"All the more reason to start immediately." He pointed toward the chair directly across from the podium. "You sit there, so I can see you. I want you to listen very carefully." He touched his ear. "You need to start writing in a journal." He waved his pen.

Writing. Once treatment started, the habit disappeared. Cassidy no longer woke up early to write poems or scribble down his thoughts at the start of each day. Now he slept in as long as he could. The blank page glowered like an enemy. "I don't think I can write anymore."

"Easy." Dr. Chang handed him a pen and a notebook. "You open up to a fresh sheet and put down words from the heart." Nodding, he knocked a closed fist against his chest. "No one will read the notebook unless you want to share with the group." He offered Cassidy a stack of books from a shelf underneath the podium. "Don't worry about taking notes during lecture. Everything we say is in these books." When he smiled, his eyes disappeared above his apple cheeks. "When times get hard, remember I've treated thousands of patients. No one ever relapsed who took what I said to heart."

Cassidy hugged the stack of books against his chest and heaved a sigh. Twelve weeks of listening to this little man with the squinty eyes and big cheeks talk about not drinking. Twelve weeks of abstinence. Twelve weeks of meetings. *I can do twelve weeks*. He swallowed, and the pain in his throat throbbed. *I just don't know if I can do a lifetime.*

****

Deb figured since Cassidy was attending classes, group therapy, and individual counseling at Path to Hope Recovery Center, all of their problems were solved. But during her weekly trip to the church to launder the soiled altar cloths, she glimpsed Father Anthony refilling the holy water in the vestibule. A rash of fear broke out on her arms.

"How are you today, Deb?" He poured the water into the shallow dish.

The light of kindness in his eyes blistered against

her skin. She averted her gaze. A deep shame itched against the nape of her neck. Why couldn't she just trust God with everything? When surrender provided release, why doubt, question, and wonder? "Fine, Father. Thank you, and you?"

"Eager for the end of ordinary time. Advent is my favorite time of year."

She nodded, thinking of Advent, which started just after Thanksgiving. She wondered if she would have anything to be thankful for or if she would be wearing a gown of mourning. She adjusted the laundry basket against her hip. "I've always preferred Easter."

"Ah, yes, the Resurrection." He nodded, closing the empty water bottle. "Well, without birth, there could be no death."

Tension tightened like screws against her jaw. Couldn't one day go by without someone mentioning life and death? She gripped the laundry basket and lifted her chin. "I need to get these home. Goodbye, Father."

"Goodbye. Please give my love to Cassidy and Adam."

"I will." She barreled out of the church and skipped down the steps, the basket jarring against her side. A breeze blew a table runner out of the basket. The green material flapped, landing on one of the stairs. Stooping, she picked up the coarse material.

"Fancy meeting you here." Elliot knelt beside her. "Need help?" He gestured toward the overflowing basket.

"No, thank you." When she wanted to be alone, why was he always around? She glanced over his shoulder at the parking lot that suddenly seemed so far away.

"I've missed you at the altar society meetings." He squinted in the sunlight. "Have you been ill?"

"No." The monosyllabic response deterred further questions. She stood, shifting the basket to the other hip.

"I heard about Cassidy passing out at Jasper's." He shook his head and spread his arms wide. "When I hear those types of stories, I think about not renewing our liquor license."

"You're not responsible for my husband's actions." She pivoted to walk around him.

He stepped in front of her and lifted the basket out of her grasp. "I've informed my staff not to serve him if he shows up again."

The sunlight caught the stubble against his chin, and a fire of gold and red flared up his cheeks.

"You don't need any trouble." He followed down the steps.

Bowing her head, she resisted the urge to seize the basket and run to her car. Something about his unsolicited help comforted her, and she softened her reluctance. Maybe he wasn't a complete scoundrel like Geraldine made him out to be. Maybe he was truly concerned about her and her family in a brotherly way. She dropped her shoulders and lengthened her steps. When was the last time she could depend on a man other than Cassidy?

Heat rippled up from the pavement and collided with the cool breeze, hinting at a change in the season. Cassidy's disease, on the other hand, stretched ahead like an endless summer. Even after his last checkup, the doctor couldn't reassure them the treatment was successful. No one would know until after the PET scan after the final dose of chemo in October.

"I hope you don't mind but I've been praying for you and your family." Elliot stopped by the trunk of her four-door sedan. "Can you come by Jasper's tonight between six and seven? I'll have a meal ready for your family, no charge."

Suspicion braided across her shoulders. Why was he being so generous? Did he feel guilty Cassidy passed out at his establishment? From her pocket, she squeezed the button on the key fob to unlock the trunk.

Elliot positioned the basket inside and clicked the trunk closed. "Do you guys like fish and chips?"

"Cassidy's on a feeding tube." She twirled the house key on the metal ring.

He tilted his smile. "I'm talking about you and the boy."

"Adam?" She lifted her voice, an octave higher than necessary.

He chuckled, and his green eyes narrowed into slits. "Yes, a meal for Adam and you."

Thinking, she frowned. She had not been to Jasper's since Geraldine's brush with infidelity, and she had no intention of patronizing the place again. But the exhaustion of caring for both Adam and Cassidy sagged against her shoulders, and the prospect of cooking in this unbearable heat felt like yet another punishment for sins she could not shake.

Clasping his hands in front of his thighs, he waited.

Was his offer genuine or tainted by an ulterior motive?

Being a woman of faith, she decided to trust him. "Okay. I'll be there at six-thirty."

"Good." Nodding, he widened his smile. "I look forward to seeing you, sister."

She stepped away. The nickname of *my sober saint* had been replaced with *sister*. During Mass, Father Anthony often referred to the congregation as his family and addressed everyone as his brother or sister. Did Elliot view her as a sister in faith? "Thank you."

"My pleasure." He turned back toward the church. In the blazing heat, he shuffled with his hands thrust into his pockets, his head bent toward the ground, and his shoulders rounded.

What burden other than his late wife's death did he carry? Was he trying to make up for his indiscretion with Geraldine? What was his motive other than kindness? She rubbed her hands along the length of her arms, and the rash of fear resurfaced. Scratching her skin, she wondered if she misplaced her trust.

Chapter Eighteen

Cassidy sat on the recliner, listening to music through his headphones. Closing his eyes, he relaxed into the comforting rhythms of the acoustic song. The whir of the ceiling fan cooled his face. Since beginning the outpatient program, he noticed stabilization in his temperament and an improvement in his energy levels. No longer wildly moody or unable to keep his eyes open, he functioned more or less like a sick man with a low-grade fever—slow and wavering but not incapacitated.

Dr. Rodriguez had not released him to play softball or return to work.

Dr. Chang still encouraged him to bring Deb to his family counseling sessions, even though Cassidy wasn't ready to open up about anything.

He preferred to sit on the recliner and meditate, losing himself in the moment. As he breathed in deeply for a count of four and held his breath for a count of seven, he visualized the tumor shrinking and the sores disappearing from the roof of his mouth and along the gum lines. Exhaling, he imagined tasting food again and swallowing without pain.

"Dad."

His son's voice punctured the vision like a pinprick to a balloon. Cassidy startled, blinking open his eyes.

Adam tugged his arm. "Play."

"Not right now, buddy." In the watery aftermath of a broken meditation, Cassidy glanced around, looking for Deb. Where was she? "I need to rest."

"No. Play." Adam climbed onto Cassidy's lap. His knee nudged the exposed feeding tube.

Cassidy wrenched in pain. "Deb!" The shout for help shook his body. He flailed beneath his son's arms and legs. "Buddy, be careful. You're hurting Daddy."

"Play." Adam bounced up and down on his father's lap.

The jarring movement jabbed his stomach muscles. He raised his head and stared at the empty doorway. When he needed his wife, where was she? Another sharp pain shot through his side from Adam's bony knee. "Deb!"

"I'm coming!" She ran into the room, carrying a load of laundry in her arms. Widening her eyes, she tossed the linens on the sofa and yanked Adam's arm. "Get off your father."

"Move his knee." Cassidy winced. "He's twisting the feeding tube."

Deb grabbed Adam's leg and tugged.

Adam slid off his father's lap. Turning, he lurched at Deb. Fists pummeled her shoulders and chest. "Dad. Play."

Raising her arms to cover her face, Deb ducked. "No, your father can't play. He needs his rest."

Why can't she handle him? Irritation shattered Cassidy's patience. He stood, writhing in pain. *Why can't he respect her?* He shoved Adam by the shoulder. "Stop beating up your stepmom." He pointed toward the doorway. "Go to your room."

Tipping back his head, Adam wailed.

The scream shot through Cassidy's head like an arrow. He cupped his hands over his ears. His stomach already hurt where Adam's knee had been. Now a headache bruised his skull. "I can't take this chaos anymore, Deb." He lowered his hands into fists, searching for his phone. "We need to call Stephanie and ask her to take him full-time until treatment is over. I need peace."

Deb widened her eyes and took a step forward. "No one's calling that woman." She seized Adam's arm with one hand and pointed toward the doorway with the other. "Go to your room. Get your shoes. We'll go for a car ride and pick up dinner, okay?"

Adam lowered his arms and whimpered. "Eat?"

"Yes, we'll eat after the car ride." A muscle twitched in her jaw. "Now, go get your shoes."

Adam disappeared.

After heaving a sigh, Cassidy lifted his shirt and examined the plastic tubing, which seemed intact in spite of the abuse. The muscles of his stomach tensed, and he touched the skin tender enough to bruise. Next time, he might not be so lucky. Adam might dislodge the feeding tube. Then Cassidy would end up in the emergency room to get the tube reinserted. The prospect filled him with dread. He lowered his shirt and ran his fingers through the curls on his head. "I think we should go to family counseling."

"Counseling?" Deb threw up her arms. "You're the one who's sick. The rest of us are fine."

"We're not fine." As Cassidy spoke, he winced from the pain. He waved a hand between them. Sadness chilled his body. When he'd married Deb, he'd promised himself he wouldn't let his second marriage end. He wanted a stronger, better union. Regardless of the effort. But did Deb? He blinked against the gritty feeling in his eyes. "We're falling apart."

Huffing, she placed her hands on her hips and broadened her stance. "Are you saying I'm not a good wife and stepmother?"

He rubbed his forehead. He was tired of fighting with Deb and wrestling with Adam. Maybe he should have asked Dr. Rodriguez for a referral to an inpatient treatment program. The thought of being alone in a room with nothing but silence suddenly seemed appealing. "No, I'm not saying you're a bad wife and stepmother. I'm saying we need help." He strode over to the window and gazed out at the apple tree. Last weekend, Lionel and Nick came over and plucked the ripe fruit from the tree and mowed the lawn. Cassidy glanced over his shoulder and pointed toward the yard. "What's wrong with asking for help?"

Deb shook her head. "Having the guys take care of the yard is completely different than having Stephanie take care of Adam."

"Why shouldn't she take care of him?" Cassidy opened his arms. "He's her son."

Adam wandered into the room, holding his shoes. "Go."

For a long moment, Deb glowered at Cassidy. She snatched the shoes out of Adam's hands and pointed toward the sofa full of laundry. "Sit."

Adam plunked down on the sofa, and the clean linen tumbled onto the floor.

Sighing, Deb bit her lower lip and knelt. She slipped on one shoe and then the other. With her small fingers, she tied the laces. Standing, she nudged Adam toward the doorway. "Say bye to your father. We'll be back in a little while."

"Bye." Adam flipped his hand before bolting out of the room.

As soon as the front door clicked shut, Cassidy turned toward the window.

Deb struggled to get Adam into the backseat of the four-door sedan.

Adam tugged the seatbelt across his chest, his head dipped in concentration. When the seatbelt didn't snap into place, he released it and bit his fingers.

Without giving him time to calm down and try again, Deb yanked the seatbelt across his body and snapped it into place.

She's parenting all wrong. Tension pulsed in his temples. Unlike Deb, Cassidy would have waited a few minutes, giving his son ample time to succeed. From experience, Adam needed several attempts to buckle his seatbelt. But Deb didn't have the patience.

In his hand, the cell phone felt as cold and heavy as a gun. He waited until Deb drove away before he called Stephanie.

****

Turning up the volume on the radio, Deb drove through the streets of downtown toward Jasper's Bar and Grill. High-rise luxury hotels crammed next to designer boutiques. Summer tourists lingered on the sidewalks. In Courthouse Square, a big band played live music. The clock tower chimed six-thirty. Traffic slowed to a crawl.

Adam kicked the back of her seat with his big feet.

She bit her lower lip, resisting the urge to glance into the rearview mirror and yell, demanding him to stop. Tension from the disagreement with Cassidy knotted her neck and shoulders. Counseling? Why did she need to go to counseling when she wasn't sick or drinking? She just needed a little extra help around the house, not Stephanie taking Adam away for a handful of weeks.

Driving past Courthouse Square, she slowed and searched for parking. The handicap spot in front of Jasper's was open. She steered into the slot and hung the placard on the rearview mirror. Leaving the music playing, she plunged a hand into her purse and rooted around for her phone. After dialing the bar's phone number, she waited.

"Jasper's Bar and Grill, Elliot speaking."

His voice sounded deep and throaty against the cacophony of conversation, the click of glasses, and the clash of silverware. She took a deep breath, her fingers trembling against the phone. "Hi, it's Deb. I'm outside in handicap parking with Adam."

"Wonderful."

The delightful tone of his voice uplifted her spirits, and she smiled.

"I'll be right out."

She ended the call and waited, glancing every now and then into the rearview mirror to check on Adam who just bobbed his head to the beat of the drum solo.

The doors to the bar opened, and Elliot squinted in the sunlight, carrying two bags of food.

Deb popped the trunk and opened her door to help him. A rush of cool air breathed against her skin, reminding her fall was right around the corner.

"No need to get out."

Ignoring his comment, she strode toward the back

of the car and lifted the door to the trunk. "If you place the food inside the car, Adam will eat everything before we get home."

He arranged the bags in the space, stepped back, and raised a finger. "Wait a second. Let me get a cardboard box, so the food won't slide around."

"Good idea." She flashed a smile. While she waited, she closed her eyes and breathed in the crisp scent of fish and chips.

The bell against the door jangled, and Elliot hustled toward her with a cardboard box. He rearranged everything again before closing the trunk. "There. Now you shouldn't have a problem getting the food home safely."

Blinking in the waning sunlight, Deb clasped her hands together. "Thank you again."

"My pleasure." He glanced up and down the length of her body and frowned. "You look like you've had a rough day."

Averting her gaze, she swallowed against the tightness in her throat. "Cass and I had a fight. He wants his ex-wife to take care of Adam until his treatment is done."

"Sounds like a good plan."

She gnawed on her lower lip. "I don't think he'd ask her to take care of him if I was a better wife and stepmother."

"Ah, now don't go blaming yourself for anything." Shaking his head, he flicked a wrist. "You're doing the best you can. Cancer is a savage beast. It will destroy everything you love if you let it. Be grateful and accept the help."

She stared, her feet rooted to the pavement. Maybe

Elliot was right. She should abandon her stance against Stephanie and join forces for the wellbeing of her family. "Thanks for the advice." She jangled her keys. "I need to get home and feed Adam."

"Enjoy the meal." Smiling, he stepped onto the sidewalk. "I hope you'll come again. Bring your husband. We'll celebrate the return of his health."

"How can you be so hopeful when you lost your wife to this disease?" She stood beside the driver's door, her fingers on the handle. Already the cool breath of a foggy night traveled on a slight breeze.

He shrugged. "What's the alternative? Despair?"

Bowing her head, she opened the door and slipped into the car. Strumming guitars rattled the windows. "Thanks again."

"You're welcome, sister." He stood on the sidewalk and lifted a hand goodbye.

After backing up, she shifted gears and glanced at Elliot.

He turned toward the double glass doors of his restaurant with the same slope to his shoulders, his head dipped toward the ground, and his feet shuffling.

She steered into the lane heading back toward her home. Soothing warmth spread across her chest and down her arms. She whistled along with the song on the radio, a catchy tune she couldn't name. Rolling down the window, she let the cooling breeze ruffle her short hair. A smile lingered at the corners of her lips, thinking of the sustenance in the trunk, and the luxury of not cooking. A sharp jab poked her chest. Oh, when would she finally acknowledge Elliot for whom he was—a fallible and kindhearted friend?

Chapter Nineteen

Cassidy tucked the phone into his front pocket. He wondered if Deb would be back by the time Stephanie arrived to pick up Adam. When he called a few minutes ago, he was calm and matter-of-fact. "I need help. Can you take Adam until my treatment is over?" Thankfully, she didn't ask any questions or put up a fight, unlike his current wife. He tensed his jaw and stared out the window, waiting for the four-door sedan to round the bend of the cul-de-sac and lumber into the driveway. He sighed and turned away. Oh, why did he leave one woman for another? What made him think trading wives would solve anything?

Sitting on the recliner, he clasped his hands between his knees and wondered about those final years with Stephanie colliding with his affair with Deb. How being with Deb was an escape from the problems at home—the loss of a son who could never play softball and the disappointment of a wife who would never be content as a housewife and mother but who yearned for something he could not understand or provide. He never examined his relationship with Deb, the dynamics outside their illicit time together, how his atheism clashed with her faith, and how his need for autonomy rammed into her need for control. He also never examined how he drowned any potential conflict with one beer after another until the edges of his thoughts

139

blurred into a smear of nothingness. Now, without the balm of booze, he was left with the nakedness of his problems.

From the coffee table, he grabbed his notebook and pen and began writing his thoughts. All the experiences of his life, which he carried like unopened boxes from year to year, he slowly unpacked through free-flowing words. His feelings about his son, his first marriage to Stephanie, his second marriage to Deb, his construction business, his softball buddies, and his lifelong friends spooled out onto the page. Calm settled over him, and a sense of peace expanded in his chest. Writing, even if it wasn't poetry, felt freeing again.

The slam of a car door stopped him mid-sentence, and he reluctantly closed the notebook. Standing, he glanced out the window.

Deb held open the back door of the sedan.

Adam released the seatbelt and climbed out of the car, tottering up to the porch.

Cassidy met him in the foyer. "How was the ride, buddy?"

"Eat." Adam disappeared into the kitchen.

A few moments later, Deb arrived, carrying a cardboard box full of salty-smelling fried foods.

How could she consider fast food dinner? He cringed, keeping his mouth shut. Even Stephanie could whip up a quick, vegetable stir fry no matter how hassled she was. "Need help?" he asked, glancing at the box in her arms.

"No, thank you. Just go into the other room and rest. I'll feed Adam."

The sternness in her voice chastised him. He locked the front door, padded back into the living room, and sat in his recliner. He grabbed the notebook and pen and turned to the unfinished page. Where was he? Fear and anticipation rattled his nerves. Unable to focus, he closed the notebook and trained his gaze on the window, waiting for a black pickup truck to power around the bend. How many years had it been since he actually looked forward to seeing his ex-wife?

****

Deb hovered over the kitchen table. On a plastic dinner plate, she cut up fried fish and scooped out greasy fries. Every few seconds, she batted away Adam's hand while she worked. The heavy scent of grease, salt, and cod filled the room. A layer of sweat creased her forehead in spite of the cool air blowing through the open window above the kitchen sink. Sunlight slanted across the floor and illuminated the table. Bending over Adam, she raised his hand and made the sign of the cross. "Bless us, O Lord, and these thy gifts…" She finished the prayer before she shoveled a crisp piece of fish into his open mouth.

Ding-DONG!

Who is here? Frowning, Deb grabbed the plate and swerved away from the kitchen table.

"Eat." Adam stood, knocking over the chair.

Deb swiveled. "Wait." Glancing over her shoulder, she narrowed her gaze. "I'll be right back." She pivoted toward the hall.

"Don't bother." Cassidy shuffled into the foyer, holding the feeding container in one hand, his other hand on the doorknob. "Go feed Adam."

From the kitchen, Adam howled.

Torn between curiosity and duty, Deb ducked back into the kitchen and set the chair upright. Gesturing toward Adam, she sat and placed the plate on the table. She handed him a crispy fry.

As soon as he sat, he seized the fry out of her hand and folded it into his mouth.

Voices murmured through the wall. Deb tilted her head, straining to hear who the visitor might be.

Adam lurched for the plate.

"No." With one swift motion, she held the plate out of his reach. "Sit." She pointed toward the table. "Hands down and wait."

Whimpering, Adam complied.

Deb offered him another fry, then a mouthful of fish and a sip from a glass of water. She fell into a rhythm, working through the meal, while her own plate cooled on the kitchen counter by the stove. She leaned forward, sliding her chair closer to the wall. The sounds of a woman's voice mingled with Cassidy's throaty growl. Hitching her breath, she widened her eyes and clamped her fingers tight around the fork. Her movements stiffened into a mechanical motion, feeding Adam the last bits of the meal.

Finished, Adam leaned back against the chair and tapped his fingers against the table. "Cookie." He grinned.

Deb stood and gathered the plate, fork, and glass. "Okay. Just a minute." After setting the dishes in the sink, she rinsed the grease and salt from her fingers and dried her hands on a dish towel. From the top shelf of a cabinet, she stretched on her toes and tapped the edge of a box of cookies until it tumbled into her arms. She removed a chocolate chip cookie and broke it in half, offering a piece to Adam.

He plucked the cookie out of her fingers and thrust

it into his mouth. "More."

"Wash your hands first."

Standing side-by-side at the sink, Deb soaped up his slender hands and rinsed them with warm water. The freckled skin reminded her of Cassidy. When was the last time she held his hand? She couldn't remember. She turned off the faucet and rubbed Adam's hands dry with a dish cloth. Smiling, she handed him the other half of the cookie. "Good job eating."

"Thank you." He crumpled the cookie into his mouth and bolted for the doorway.

Sighing with exhaustion, Deb wrung her hands in the dish towel and followed him.

"Hey, buddy. Look who's here." Cassidy waved toward the woman standing in the living room.

Adam glanced and waved. "Bye-bye." He loped down the hall to his room and shut the door.

Standing in the doorway to the living room, Deb glimpsed the visitor—Stephanie. Every nerve in Deb's fingers tingled with anger. She choked the dish towel. How dare Stephanie arrive uninvited during dinner time? And why did she always appear so perfect? This evening she was dressed in a clean T-shirt and skinny jeans, her auburn hair recently cropped short and styled into a single wave. She looked so smug standing next to Cassidy by the sofa, grinning like she won a jackpot. Bitterness throbbed against Deb's temples, and her jaw twitched. "What are you doing here?"

With her thumb, Stephanie gestured toward Cassidy. "He called and asked me to take Adam for a few weeks."

"A few weeks?" Deb gaped and wrung the dish towel in her hands. "We don't need help."

"*I* need help." Cassidy lifted the feeding container in his hand. "You can't be expected to do everything."

"And she can?" Deb trembled, her voice rising to a dangerous pitch. "Adam isn't *that* hard." The lie tugged like fatigue in her arms and legs.

Cassidy pursed his lips. "You can't manage your volunteer work, Adam, the household, and me."

Opening her arms, Stephanie took a step forward. "I'm happy to take Adam. He's the reason why I left LA."

The skin bristled at the back of Deb's neck. She seethed, gritting her teeth. All this time, she believed Cassidy appreciated her efforts to parent Adam and care for his needs. But Cassidy was just biding time, waiting until the tasks appeared to be too much, before calling his ex-wife to the rescue. Deb pointed toward the window. "Go back to LA. I never asked for you to come here."

"You're right." Stephanie dropped her arms to the sides, straightened her spine, and lifted her chin. "Cassidy did."

With a sidelong glance at her husband, Deb took a deep breath. "I am handling everything just fine."

"No, you're not." Cassidy pointed toward his stomach. A blue-and-purple bruise blossomed around the tubing. "Adam's out of control. You're not strong enough or experienced enough to handle his outbursts."

Deb held her breath, her pulse beating wildly in her throat. "I am a good stepmom."

"Of course, you are." Stephanie grinned and nodded.

The patronizing gesture fanned the fury growing in her gut. Deb released her breath and stabbed a hand into her pocket, searching for her rosary beads.

Cassidy crossed the living room and touched her shoulder with his other hand. "Please, don't take this opportunity the wrong way."

Opportunity? What was so opportune about his ex-wife taking her stepson for a few weeks? Deb bristled, stepping back, and letting his hand fall away. In her pocket, she rubbed her fingers across the worn beads, but no comfort reassured her.

"Uncle John and I would love to spend time with him." Stephanie pointed toward the ceiling. "I bought a new sound system for Adam's music with speakers in every room."

Deb buckled her knees and sank onto the sofa. "Adam likes his computer tablet." She stared at Cassidy's slippers and Stephanie's heels. They seemed so composed and so perfectly functional together—a team without her. She sobbed, tears squeezing out of her eyes and dribbling down her cheeks.

"See." Cassidy touched her shoulder. "You need a break."

"No, I don't." She raised her head and her voice. "I'm upset because *she's* here." She jabbed a finger toward Stephanie. "Where was she when we got married and wanted to go on a honeymoon?" She narrowed her gaze at Cassidy. "In LA. Where was she when I wanted to go with you to the World Masters last year? In LA." She thumbed her finger toward the doorway. "She needs to go back to LA."

"How dare you tell me where I need to be?" Stephanie thrust her face toward Deb and ticked off each complaint on her fingers. "You stole my husband from me. You broke up my family. You need to go back to the closet."

"Closet?" Deb stood, frowning. She wasn't hiding from anyone. "I was never in the closet."

Scoffing, Stephanie shook her head and folded her arms over her chest. "The cloister."

"Cloister?" Deb fumed. "Get your words right." How could Cassidy, a poet, have chosen a woman who didn't know the definition of words? "I lived in a *convent* before I moved here." She heaved her shoulders and nodded toward Cassidy. "I've been released from that life. I belong here, with him. We're married."

Stephanie grimaced. "You never had a child with him."

True, but why did that fact matter when she was caring for Adam as if he was her own flesh and blood? Deb tossed the dish towel on the coffee table and clenched her fists. "You left Cassidy to go to LA to pursue your acting career. If you wanted Adam, you would have stayed and fought for your rights as a mother."

Cassidy wedged between the women. "Please, let's not fight."

"Too late." Deb spat. "You instigated this argument by inviting this woman into my home." She stomped a foot.

"I'll leave." Stephanie stalked out of the room and down the hallway. "Adam, get your shoes. We're going for a car ride."

Breathing hard, Deb glanced at the empty feeding container in Cassidy's hand. How had their relationship devolved into this mess? "I can't believe you think so little of me when I gave up everything to be with you."

He glowered. "I never asked you to sacrifice anything. You volunteered."

"I didn't want to be your mistress." Deb gulped, blotting her moist face with the palm of her hands. She sniffled, recalling how guilty she felt enjoying the pleasure of being in a married man's arms. "I only wanted to be your wife."

"Well, congratulations. You succeeded." He lifted an arm, punching the air with a fist.

The victory tasted bitter in her mouth. She swiveled and stomped out of the room. In the hallway, she collided with Stephanie and Adam. Seeing mother and son side-by-side, she noticed the resemblance—the same slender build, the same slight smile, and the same defiant glint in the eyes. Why did nature trump nurture? Deb shoved back her shoulders and steeled her heart, not wanting to break apart again. "Be good for your mom and Uncle Johnny." Deb kissed Adam's cheek. "Don't forget to say goodbye to your dad."

Adam wandered into the living room.

Stephanie remained in the hall and narrowed her gaze. "You can go to the World Masters this year." She pursed her lips. "Start planning that honeymoon for next year, because you will go. I'll take Adam. You just tell me when."

Deb flinched. How could she plan for next year? Next year Cassidy might not even be alive. "I can't. We're already married."

"Never too late for a honeymoon." Stephanie crossed her arms over her chest and tapped a foot. "I waited over twenty years to break into a hit series. You haven't waited that long, have you?" Without staying for a response, she nudged past Deb and grabbed

Adam's hand.

Deb followed them into the foyer and closed the front door after they left. An engine revved in the driveway, and her heartbeat thudded inside the cage of her chest. *He's gone*. Even though she wanted to complain, the calm of a childless household echoed with relief. She strode back into the empty living room before padding into the kitchen.

Cassidy stood at the sink, flushing water through the feeding tube. His back hunched, and his shoulders slumped.

Oh, how gaunt and shapeless he appeared. A pang of terror ricocheted down her legs and into her feet, grounding her to the space beside him. "Do you need help?"

Without turning to face her, he shook his head. "Why don't you eat? I'm sure you're hungry."

The pit in her stomach clenched like a tight fist. Even if she wanted to, she couldn't eat. The weight of the argument still hung heavy in the cool breeze from the open window. The scent of fish and chips was nothing but a greasy smear lingering around the edges. She leaned against the counter.

Cassidy cleaned and dried the skin around the tube.

The bruise bloomed like a dead rose. Guilt and regret hovered around her, a halo of misery. She clutched her waist and bent forward, staring at her feet. "I'm sorry."

"Don't be."

His voice sounded tired and faraway. She lifted her face and studied his profile. The skin around his jowls sagged. He appeared old, worn down, and defeated. No wonder he drank. To forget. To escape. To pretend everything was all right even though nothing was all right and possibly never would be again.

"I know you both love me, and I know you both hate each other." He flicked a glance in her direction. "I should have known that combination would have caused a cat fight." He huffed. "Nick keeps bugging me to finalize my estate planning. I need you both to help me setup Adam's special needs trust. How can I accomplish that task if you two can't be in the same room?"

Another knot of guilt tightened in her chest. She considered confessing tonight's transgressions in the Sacrament of Reconciliation. What penance would Father Anthony give?

"If you want to be angry with anyone, you should be angry with me." Cassidy met her gaze. "I initiated an affair with you, knowing I was married. I had no intention of ending anything with anyone, and look where I am." He pointed to his throat. "I caused all this heartache between two good women, both of whom I don't deserve." He coughed and winced. "I'm the culprit, not Stephanie. Don't hate her. Hate me."

She softened, curling toward him. The pain was palpable, as thick as the taste of fog in the damp air. With one hand, she shut the window. Afterward, she let her fingers travel to the back of his hand gripping the edge of the sink. The skin was coarse and freckled, an older version of Adam. All those early feelings of tenderness and love flooded her. "I can't hate you."

"Then stop hating her. She's only helping us."

Be grateful and accept the help. Elliot's advice hovered between them, like an admonishment. She dipped her chin to her chest. Oh, how could she learn to take those words to heart? Straightening her spine, she lifted her chin. "Okay. I will."

"Are you sure?" He lurched away, releasing his grip from the edge of the counter. "Do you promise not to attack her the next time she offers assistance?"

She cringed at his glower. Could she control her emotions instead of reacting the same way she always did? "I'll try."

"Trying isn't good enough. You either will, or you won't."

Her thoughts snagged on a phrase. *Good enough.* She stiffened, feeling lightning bolts of anger rip through her body. When would she ever be good enough?

The silence echoed like a thudding heartbeat in the room.

Cassidy shook his head and turned away. "I'll be in the living room if you need me. Enjoy your dinner."

Alone, she stood at the counter, thinking about Stephanie's promise to care for Adam through the World Masters and next year through a long-awaited honeymoon. Could she dare to hope and plan that far into the future? Bowing her head, she silently prayed. *God, please let me believe we will be in a better place this time next year.* She sighed. *And please grant me the strength to welcome Stephanie's help.*

Chapter Twenty

A couple of days later, Cassidy sat next to Deb in Dr. Chang's office for their first family therapy session. The room was small and cozy with framed prints of flowers on the white walls and the scent of pine and old paper from the built-in bookcase next to the window overlooking the parking lot. Cassidy shifted in the overstuffed chair and smiled at Dr. Chang, who sat across a large desk occupied only by a box of tissues and a phone. With Adam's absence, the constant stress between him and Deb escalated to shouting matches and voids of silence. Each day, a sense of alienation drove them further apart. Finally, Cassidy mentioned the possibility of counseling. He didn't expect Deb to agree.

But here she was, sitting next to him in another overstuffed chair, rubbing her rosary beads. Frowning, Cassidy wished she was holding his hand.

Dr. Chang crossed an ankle over his knee and leaned back in the creaky office chair. "Who would like to begin?"

After a quick glance at his wife, Cassidy nodded. Since starting treatment, he wrote about his thoughts and feelings. The words flowed smoothly, effortlessly like water from a running faucet until he focused on his wife. Then the words dried up. How could he describe the dead-end nothingness he felt around her? He clutched his hands. Sweat beaded on the back of his neck. "I feel like I've fallen out of love."

Deb gaped, dropping the rosary beads into her lap. "Am I here so you can end our marriage?" With wide eyes, she shifted to face him. "I thought you wanted to work on our relationship."

Cassidy frowned. Why was she reacting this way? Wasn't she supposed to grow curious and ask him to tell her more just like the other patients did during group therapy? He pointed a finger at Dr. Chang. "You said to tell her how I feel. I did. What comes next?" Without waiting for a response, he raised a hand and curled a finger toward his palm. "I've given up alcohol. I've given up softball. I've given up work. I've given up Adam." He choked and curled the last finger to make a fist. "I've given up my health." Shaking his head from side to side, he lowered his arm. "I'm not here to give up anything else." He turned to Deb and groped for her hand. "Especially not you."

Frowning, she lowered her gaze, tugged away her fingers, and grabbed her rosary beads. "Why keep me around if you don't love me anymore?"

Frustration tensed Cassidy's jaw. How could he explain what he wanted conflicted with how he felt without alienating his wife any further?

Dr. Chang lifted a hand. "Sometimes when we're overwhelmed by circumstances, we pull back instead of reach out." He gazed at Cassidy and offered a small smile. "When we're faced with a life-threatening illness, we stop caring. Apathy allows us to detach, regroup, and restore the balance we've lost from being sick."

Scowling, Deb leaned forward. "Are you saying he

doesn't love me because he's battling cancer?"

"Possibly." Dr. Chang met her gaze for a moment before glancing at Cassidy. "Before your diagnosis, how did you feel about Deb?"

Cassidy shrugged. "I don't know. We just went about our routine. Everything was fine. I didn't have to think or feel anything."

Dr. Chang raised his eyebrows. "You avoided your relationship through work, alcohol, sports, Adam, and poetry." He uncurled his fingers one at a time.

"Poetry?" Deb snickered. "He hasn't written since he self-published his book of poems two Christmases ago."

"Maybe poetry is the solution and not the problem." Dr. Chang steepled his fingers. "Have you been journaling any poetry?"

"Not poetry." Those musical lines and brilliant images no longer flowed from Cassidy's pen. He shrugged. "Just thoughts and feelings as they surface." Whenever he found words to describe the chaos inside of him, a sense of calm quieted the internal storm. The pressure in his chest released, and the fears dissolved. Words anchored and freed him. He stared at his callous-free fingers. Poet's hands, not construction worker's hands. For the first time since high school, the nail beds were clean and the pads of his fingers were smooth. He stretched his fingers, aching for the woodsy smell of lumber, the buzz of saws, the whack of nails, and the satisfaction of watching a building rise from the dirt.

Writing was a lot like construction—laying one word after another, erecting a story from the ground of his thoughts. But poetry was different. Those rhyming lines sounded more like music. He sighed. "I don't

153

write poems. I just jot down whatever comes to mind—nothing formal." The words, once bright and hopeful with lyricism, twisted into darkness and despair. Why share those thoughts with anyone?

"Did poetry connect you both before the diagnosis?" Dr. Chang asked.

Deb nodded. "We both used to write. I'm more private than Cassidy. I don't publish. He's always been more ambitious." Smiling, she glanced at her husband. "He used to show me his poetry once a week and ask me to critique it." A divot formed between her eyebrows. "You haven't asked for my opinion in months."

The sad longing in her voice strangled him. "Why share my darkness?" He hardened the line of his mouth. "I don't want you judging me." Since his diagnosis, Deb ranted and raved over every little thing he did.

She tucked her hands in her armpits and lowered her head. "I don't judge."

"Yes, you do." He slapped his thighs. "I don't sleep enough. I don't relax enough. I don't walk enough." His throat burned. "I'm tired of not being enough."

After shifting toward him, she tapped her fingers against her chest. "Why is everything my fault? I'm not a good stepmother. I don't parent Adam like you do. I volunteer too much at the church." Blinking, she sniffed. "I love you more than God. I left Him to be with you, and now you don't love me anymore." Her voice broke into a sob.

Cassidy seized a tissue and stuffed it into her hand. He hated hearing her cry almost as much as he hated crying. The emptiness expanded in his chest, and the feeling of nothingness filled all of his muscles. "You're not the only one who left someone. I betrayed Stephanie." He remembered the time he called Stephanie to share his diagnosis and how surprised he was when she told him how she felt. "She still loves me. She always has and always will." The truth wedged between them.

Deb dabbed her eyes and huffed. "Did you fall out of love with her, too?"

He flinched from the look of venom in her gaze. "I—don't—know." He never pondered why he left one woman for the other. The transition happened so abruptly. He didn't have time to consider anything. The whirlwind of emotions he felt for Deb at the beginning when she returned to Vine Valley to care for her mother swept all reasoning from his mind. He dove deep into the deception, sneaking moments with her at every opportunity. The rush of excitement blotted out the reality of his life. He shuddered. Maybe what he felt toward Deb was never love. Maybe he was only pining for an escape from his marital responsibilities—that classic midlife crisis Stephanie always accused him of.

Deb crumpled the tissue in a fist and threw up her arms. "How can you not know?" She crossed her arms over her chest. "Did you ask her to return to Vine Valley because you're still in love?"

Bowing his head, he sighed. "I told you the truth. I don't know." He raised his head and glowered. "I'm not your God who knows everything."

"Listen to you both." Dr. Chang clapped his hands. "These feelings are important." He pointed to Deb. "You feel replaced by the ex-wife." He nodded toward Cassidy. "You feel inadequate against her religion." He waved a hand between them. "Both of you don't feel you deserve each other, but you do. You've let life get in the way of the love you have for one another."

Is he right? Cassidy pursed his lips and unclenched his hands. With a sidelong glance, he scanned Deb's short, dark hair, her scowling, brown eyes, her button nose, her tense lips, her sharp jaw, and her stiff, petite body. Was the void he felt his way of handling the guilt of possibly dying and leaving her alone?

****

As soon as Deb heard Dr. Chang mention life getting in the way of her and Cassidy loving each other, she felt the temperature in the room rise. Out of the corner of her eye, she glimpsed Cassidy scanning the length of her body. His solicitous glance incensed her. How dare he find her attractive? She tensed her jaw. A few minutes ago, he said he no longer loved her. Why acknowledge his presence?

She wondered if Geraldine faced this type of interrogation when she entered couples' therapy with Lionel two years ago. Did the therapist accuse her of falling out of love? Or was the therapist more sympathetic? Deb tapped a foot against the thin, industrial carpet. *I never should have left God for a man*. The same thought recycled through her mind since Cassidy's diagnosis. Would she feel the same way if he wasn't possibly dying? She nodded toward Dr. Chang. "We never had problems before cancer."

"Of course not." Dr. Chang smiled. "Cancer revealed the weaknesses in the structure of your relationship. Without it, you both might have gone years without realizing anything was wrong or missing."

Cassidy nodded. "I ignored problems in my first marriage." He sighed. "Stephanie and I never talked about our feelings. We never discussed anything serious. We just went along, assuming everything was okay." He paused, shifting to face his wife. "When I saw you again after all those years apart, I realized I gave up my dreams to have Adam. I was too old to play professional baseball, but I wasn't too old to be with you." He grasped her hand.

The shock of his cool skin against her warm fingers lurched the beating of her heart. She clutched his hand. Frustration melted away. This touch was why she left God to be with a man. She needed physical reassurance. Not necessarily sex, but tenderness. That gentle brush of the pads of his fingers along the curves of her body. That tender kiss from his lips on her mouth. All of those tiny gestures had disappeared with cancer.

Chemotherapy was dangerous, making him toxic. They couldn't share a bathroom. They couldn't share sex. They couldn't even deep kiss. Up until this moment, she didn't realize how much she missed the physical intimacy of his touch. She squeezed his hand and gazed into his hazel eyes. Her heartbeat knocked against her ribs. Oh, what would he think if she told him the truth? "I miss being close to your body. I find so much comfort in your skin." She smiled, stroking his knuckles. "My favorite part of sex is right afterward when you curl your leg over mine and tuck me close to your chest and fall asleep." With the memory, she sighed. "We haven't slept together since treatment started."

"We can't." Cassidy shook her hand. "I'm radioactive."

She laughed, squeezing his fingers. "You'd kill me quicker than kryptonite."

"I've missed your laughter." Smiling, he lifted her hand to his mouth for a quick peck.

The gesture ignited a fire down to her bones. "I love you." She leaned closer. "I miss the old you."

"Me, too." He shifted. With his other hand, he brushed away the hair from her eyes.

Dr. Chang cleared his throat. "We're out of time." He stood and gestured toward the door. "Why don't you pick up where you left off at home? Even if you can't have sex, you can enjoy each other's body in other ways."

Deb nodded, cupping her hand over Cassidy's fingers. He was the only man she ever wanted. She hoped Dr. Chang was right, and lust could trigger that old memory of love Cassidy once felt, bringing them back to each other.

Chapter Twenty-One

A couple of weeks later, Cassidy sat beneath the awning in the backyard during a barbecue Deb organized. A glass of lemonade sweated on the picnic table, untouched. The leaves on the old oak tree, their tips browned with the first hint of autumn, wafted on the gentle breeze. Glancing around the backyard, Cassidy surveyed the guests—Lionel manning the grill, Geraldine arranging the side dishes, Nick grabbing a beer, Hope making fruit salad inside the kitchen, and Deb fluttering from person to person like a hummingbird.

The rest of his teammates and employees declined the invitation. Cassidy wondered if the others felt scared or shy or awkward around him. After all, he didn't look like himself. He had lost so much weight the skin sagged around his jowls and drooped from his arms. A belt didn't hold up his jeans, so he cinched a pair of jogging pants around his waist. If he lost any more weight, he would fit into Adam's clothes. Each morning, when he shaved the coarse hairs on his concave cheeks, he didn't stare too long at his gaunt face. The feeding tube kept him alive, but not thriving. He couldn't walk around the block without losing his breath. Even without Adam around, he couldn't sleep through the night. He was a ghost of his former self.

Nick scraped the legs of a chair against the deck

and took a seat. He cracked open a can of craft-brewed, non-alcoholic beer and offered it to Cassidy. "Tastes almost like the real thing."

Cassidy waved it away. "I'll stick with the lemonade."

Tipping back the can, Nick sipped. Shrugging, he plunked the can on the table. "No buzz."

Cassidy nodded. "I didn't know how much I relied upon that buzz until it was gone." He slumped against the picnic table. "I thought drinking was just a habit, you know, like brushing your teeth." He stared off into the distance, sniffing the smoke from the barbecue. "I miss drinking. I miss softball. I miss you guys." With a sidelong glance, he smiled. "I even miss work." He cupped his hands around his mouth. "Hey, Lionel. How's the store coming along?"

Glancing over his shoulder, Lionel waved the metal spatula. "All right, I guess." He wore a white chef's apron that emphasized his beer belly. "Didn't Guillermo tell you?"

"No." Shame brushed against Cassidy's cheeks. He hadn't spoken to his general manager in weeks. He had been too weak to care. "What's wrong?"

"Air-conditioning unit's been delayed." He flipped the burgers and turned over the hot dogs on the grill.

Geraldine placed a bucket of potato salad on the picnic table. "The coolant was bad in the first unit they sent." She stood, tugging at the hemline of her shirt. "Second unit had the coil busted. We're hoping the third time is the charm."

"Sheesh." Cassidy wagged his head from side to side. "No one told me."

"What would you do, sugar?" Geraldine splayed

her fingers against her hip. "Guillermo ordered the third unit from a different manufacturer."

"He could have told me." Cassidy bowed his head, twisting his hands in his lap. "I keep forgetting to call him."

"Don't worry your pretty, little head." Geraldine bent and kissed his forehead. "We've got things under control."

Deb drifted over to the table and rested her fingers against his shoulder. "Geraldine's right. You need to focus on getting better." She pointed toward the untouched glass of lemonade. "You want water instead?"

Frowning, Cassidy waved his hands. "I'm fine." He hated the way Deb always surrounded him, doting on him like he was a child. "Just relax. Stop hovering."

"She's not hovering, sugar. I am." Geraldine nudged aside Deb, grabbed the glass of lemonade, and strode toward the house. "I'll get you a glass of water."

Hope slipped past Geraldine and set an arrangement of fruit on the table. Her long, dark fingers released the bowl, and her metal bracelets *click-clacked* against each other. After plucking a green grape from a bunch, she dangled the fruit like a talisman. "Want to try one? Fresh from our garden."

The plump, green globe smelled sugary sweet. Although Cassidy's mouth watered, he shook his head. The sores in his mouth had not completely healed, and the back of his throat felt raw. "I'm still using the feeding tube."

Hope arched an eyebrow. "Well, I brought an ancient herbal remedy for you to try after we're gone."

Lionel chuckled. "Watch out for that witchy

woman. She gave me Lover's Pie to get me horny for my wife."

The screen door slapped shut, and Geraldine hustled down the steps. "Oh, sugar. You ate so much of that meal, I thought I'd have to rush you to the hospital." She giggled, and her eyes twinkled.

Cassidy laughed. Since the meeting with Dr. Chang, he and Deb touched each other, sometimes intimately, always stopping short of the act. The tenderness and frustration left him exhausted. "I can't use Lover's Pie right now."

Nick took Hope by the hand and guided her into his lap. "Did you discover the cure for cancer, dear?"

Leaning her head against Nick's, Hope grumbled. "I wish." She touched her fingers to her throat. "I brought some sumac tincture. Gargle with it to ease the swelling in your mouth and throat."

Cassidy bowed his head, grateful for the help but also resentful for the attention given to an illness he wanted to ignore.

"Ready to eat?" Lionel placed a platter of hamburgers and hot dogs onto the table.

Cassidy grumbled. His stomach twisted with the scent of smoky meat. He was sitting at a table with his wife and his closest friends on a balmy afternoon, and he could not eat or drink anything. The air blew out of his lungs. He needed to leave or regroup. What could he talk about?

Lionel's phone rang. "Excuse me a second. Looks like the officials are calling." He stepped aside and answered the call.

Last weekend, the Vine Valley Crushers competed with several teams west of the Rockies for the title of

Western Champions. Two teams tied—the Carson City Diggers and the Vine Valley Crushers. The officials promised to review the statistics from the whole season before declaring a winner. Before Cassidy's cancer diagnosis, the Vine Valley Crushers were undefeated. Cassidy gripped his hands together, watching Lionel's expression. Would their record stand against the Carson City Diggers?

A slow grin spread across Lionel's face. "No kidding? Thanks, sir." He ended the call and pumped a fist in the air. "We won the Westerns!"

Geraldine whooped and hollered. She danced on her kitten heels and waved her hands overhead. "Here we come, Vegas!"

Nick kissed Hope and high-fived Cassidy. "Wonderful news."

"The best news." Cassidy wobbled to his feet and hugged Lionel. "Way to go, buddy."

"If we had you pitching, we wouldn't have tied." Lionel clapped Cassidy on the back. "We would have won fair and square."

Cassidy sighed, trying not to think about his ex-brother-in-law pitching in the most important game of the year. "Well, all that matters is we won."

"You guys have to come see the game." Geraldine bustled over and embraced Cassidy and Deb in a group hug. "We can't win without you."

Cassidy breathed in the heavy scent of gardenias from Geraldine's perfume. "I can't." He had already spoken with Dr. Rodriguez and Dr. Chang. He shouldn't miss any treatments, and he shouldn't be exposed to alcohol, especially around celebrations and in bars. "I have to stay, but Deb can go." He wiggled out of Geraldine's arms and nudged his wife. Some part of him wanted everyone to leave immediately. His friends' lives blinded him with joy and anticipation while darkness lurked in every corner of his mind. *Of course, they're happy. They don't know they'll someday die.* But Deb knew, and her knowledge magnified his fears.

Deb gasped, touching her fingers to her chest. "If I go, who will take care of you?"

"I'll do fine by myself." He widened his smile. Without her hovering around him like a hummingbird, he hoped he could get some much-needed sleep. "If I need help, I'll call Dr. Rodriguez or Dr. Chang." He gestured toward the group. "Go have fun with your girlfriends. You don't get out enough."

Deb bit her lower lip and blinked.

"C'mon, sugar." Geraldine tugged her hand. "We'll have so much fun. Our ceremony is the day after the tournament ends."

"And I'll be there." Hope wandered over. "The Great Spirit appointed a new leader for the tribe, so I'm free to go."

Cassidy wrapped an arm around Deb's shoulders and waved toward the group. "See, you have no excuse. Everyone is attending."

Slowly, Deb glanced around the circle of friends. "Okay. I'll go."

"Wonderful." Cassidy tugged her close and kissed her forehead. She vibrated against him like a plucked guitar string. He needed to reassure her. "Everything will be fine." Rubbing his hand up and down her arm, he smiled. "I'll be fine." He swept his gaze around the deck full of friends, and a deep pain tugged his gut. The more he was surrounded by love, the more alone he felt. *Will I ever feel fine again?*

****

From the plane's window, an oasis of glittering lights emerged from the darkness of the desert. "We're here!" Deb tapped the arm beside her, expecting to feel the coarse hairs on Cassidy's forearm. The shock of Geraldine's smooth skin jolted her out of her reverie. When Deb decided to attend the tournament, she purchased a ticket for twice the price the others paid. The seat was located at the back of the plane. After boarding, Lionel switched spots with her, so she could sit next to Geraldine. A twinge of disappointment squeezed her chest. She always imagined visiting Las Vegas with Cassidy.

Geraldine squealed. "I can't wait to show you the strip, sugar."

Having only seen images of Las Vegas on TV and the movies, Deb didn't know what to expect. As soon as she exited the airport, a veil of hot, dry air descended. She stood in a line of strangers waiting for the shuttle to the hotel. All around her people hooted and hollered, being energized by excitement or booze. She couldn't tell. After jostling up the shuttle steps, she found a seat in the back and squeezed between Hope and Geraldine. From the pocket of her purse, she found her phone and sent a text to Cassidy.

—*We're here.*—

She clasped the phone in her hands, not expecting him to respond this late into the night.

The packed shuttle swerved onto the road toward the strip. The drowsy chatter of strangers rumbled above the sputtering engine. Each time the shuttle turned left or right, she knocked against her taller friends' shoulders. The scent of Geraldine's floral perfume contrasted starkly against the homeopathic scent of Hope's natural oils.

The guys sat closer to the door dressed in their T-shirts and shorts. Their softball caps tugged low over their foreheads.

Craning her neck, she gazed out the big windows at the glittering lights, the water show, and the street entertainers. A twinge of sadness dulled the happiness she felt. This dream-come-true trip felt more like a trial run of how life would be like without her husband.

Tourists ambled up and down the sidewalks, carrying long-necked drinks in a rainbow of colors. She imagined Cassidy safe at home and away from the temptation of never-ending streams of alcohol.

A couple of bachelorette parties floated through the crowds, the brides-to-be dressed in tiaras.

She nudged Geraldine and pointed. "You better not have us dress like those women for your pre-celebration party."

Geraldine glanced out the window and snickered. "Goodness, no, I'm renewing my vows, not attracting the interest of strangers."

Hope widened her eyes. "This place looks so different at night. During the day, you'd think we were in any other big city."

Deb's phone vibrated in her hands. Startled, she swiped a finger across the screen and read the message from Cassidy.

—*Glad you arrived safely. Have a good time. Don't worry about me. I'm fine.*—

"Hey, sugar. What's wrong?" Geraldine nudged

her shoulder.

"Nothing." Deb showed her the screen. "Cassidy just responded to my text letting him know we've arrived."

Hope smiled and rubbed her forearm. "Do you miss him already?"

Actually, a part of her didn't. Not having him beside her, moping or scribbling in his notebook or watching TV or sleeping, left her feeling lighter than she had in months. Each week, she hoped to reconnect with him through their hourly counseling sessions with Dr. Chang. So far, the effort hadn't paid off. He still hadn't fallen in love with her again. Everything she attempted to awaken his affection fell flat. He didn't want her doting care or her gentle reminders. He wanted to be left alone, and she couldn't honor the request. Even after Dr. Chang suggested she attend a support group for spouses, Deb didn't feel like her problems could be solved through detaching, finding other interests, and focusing on her own life. She wanted to ground herself as a good servant of the Lord, a great stepmom to Adam, and a wonderful wife to Cassidy—nothing more and nothing less. Were those requests too much to ask? "I'm fine." Deb patted Hope's hand. "I'm looking forward to the games and the wedding."

"And the gambling and the drinking." Geraldine winked.

Deb chuckled. She didn't gamble or drink much. "Maybe I'll spend my free hours at the pool."

"Or window shopping," Hope suggested.

By the time the shuttle arrived at their hotel and casino at the far end of the strip, Deb heaved a sigh before disembarking into the dry heat of the night. Strolling through the smoky, air-conditioned lobby, she trailed behind the teammates and friends. Gawking at the gaudy decorations, from the faux Southern Gothic charm mimicking Mardi Gras to the black wrought iron balconies overlooking the black jack tables and bars, she tugged her luggage, weaving through the flashing lights on the slot machines and the cheering crowds around the roulette tables. The high-octane energy buzzed around her. Others might welcome these distractions, but not her. She already missed home.

After checking into her quiet hotel room, she drew the blackout shades. She brushed her teeth, changed into her cotton pajamas, and lay on the mattress beneath the scratchy white sheets. In the dark, with her fingers clasped around smooth rosary beads, the tide of her thoughts rushed in and drowned her in worry, far from the comfort of sleep. Rolling over, she grabbed her phone off the nightstand and typed a message to Cassidy.

—Are you awake?—

Holding the phone in her palm, she waited.

Years ago, during their affair, she sent Cassidy texts while he was home. If he was available, he would call her. If he was busy with family, he would text a frowning emoji. She would wait for minutes like she waited now, eager for a response. If her phone rang, she answered. If her phone beeped with a text, she ran a finger across the screen and grimaced at the frowning face. Not willing to risk discovery, she kept her distance. The moments between their interactions functioned more like pauses, building anticipation until they met again. For a long time, she didn't want

Cassidy to finish upgrading her mother's home. She cherished the stolen moments between installing a walk-in tub and building a wheelchair ramp. Those forbidden touches and kisses awakened all of her senses. She cradled the phone against her chest, smiling at the memories.

After several minutes of silence, she double-checked the time. Eleven-thirty. He might be sleeping. Sorrow tugged her arms, and she tucked the phone beside her pillow and tried hopelessly to sleep. Turning onto her back, she stared at the ceiling. Closing her eyes, she imagined her husband, lying on the recliner in the living room against the flicker of the TV, a rough snore wheezing from his parted lips as he slept. The fantasy flickered and blacked out, leaving her cold and alone. In spite of the glamour and excitement of the strip, she hated being so far from home.

A thud knocked against the shared wall, and her bed shuddered. She opened her eyes. A low moan penetrated the thin sheetrock. Bedsprings creaked from the room next door. She rolled over, tucking a pillow against her ears, and blotting out the sounds. *Oh, why is everyone enjoying the fruits of love except me?*

Chapter Twenty-Two

Cassidy hated being alone. The house creaked at odd hours of the day and night like an elderly person stretching. Everywhere he glanced he noticed items to be fixed, which he neglected over the years. A broken seal in the bathroom tub and a loose light fixture in the kitchen taunted him. His parents originally owned this house. After he inherited the property, he moved back in with Adam and Stephanie. Selling the house to buy something else didn't make sense. The town was booming, and housing was scarce. If he sold, he could only have purchased a new condo, which wasn't what he wanted for his growing family.

But staying in the same place wasn't the same as settling. He loved this little ranch-style house with the big front and back yards at the end of a cul-de-sac. Not because of the memories living in every room, but because of the spaciousness. Only sometimes, too much space could make him lonely like it did now.

The first day alone, he drove to chemo. The following day, he spent in the bathroom, hugging the toilet. Weak and tired, he lay on the recliner, gazing at the ceiling fan. Even the murmur of the TV in the background couldn't swipe away the solitude. Deb's bright phone call after the first round of games was won punctuated the day like a period, ending all hope of something more. As the hours melted into night, he panicked. *How can I make it through another sleepless night alone?* Instead of driving to the liquor store, he grabbed his phone and called Stephanie. "Hey, I was wondering if I could see Adam." He smiled, trying to sound casual and light.

"Sure, I can bring him over tomorrow. What time?"

She sounded brisk and professional. He missed the tone of love in her voice. He wondered if she was still bitter over the argument with Deb. Who wouldn't be? Fighting with Deb was like entering a boxing match without a warm-up. One swing could knock someone out. But Deb wasn't here. She would be gone for a couple of more days. He could relax, and be himself. "Ten o'clock. I'm usually awake and dressed by then."

"Okay. See you at ten." She ended the call without saying goodbye.

He spent a second restless night on the hard, leather recliner, imagining his reunion with his son.

The next day, a little after ten, the guttural sound of John's old pickup truck labored up the driveway.

Cassidy released the curtain in the living room, stalked through the foyer, and into the front yard with his arms flung open. "Adam!"

The young man slid out of the cab, holding onto his mother's hand. He was freshly bathed and changed, from his fluffed curls to his ironed clothes and his tied shoes.

"Come here, buddy." Cassidy wrapped his arms around Adam's shoulders, folding him close. The young man felt solid and firm. He didn't smell like the delicate floral tones of Deb's shampoo and body soap. He smelled strong and musky like a man. Stephanie must have gone shopping, buying all of Adam's favorite things, which was something Deb never did.

"Dad." Adam grabbed Cassidy's hand and lured him into the house.

Stephanie hesitated on the porch, her hands clasped in front of her body, glancing from Cassidy to Adam. "Do you want me to stay for the visit or run some errands and come back to pick him up?"

Cassidy held his son's hand. "I don't know. I just wanted to see him. I was tired of being alone." He ruffled Adam's curls. "I missed you, buddy."

Smiling, Stephanie gestured toward the foyer. "Well, I don't want to deprive you of him, but I don't want to intrude, either."

Nodding, Cassidy considered her words. She was trying to be respectful, not pushing her agenda, if she even had one. If he asked her to leave, she would go. If he asked her to stay, she might linger. Or at least, he hoped she might. "Please have lunch with us."

She creased her forehead. "Are you sure?"

He shrugged. "Why not? Deb's not here. You won't get me into trouble." He forced a laugh.

After stepping inside the house, she closed and locked the door. "Why does Deb hate me? I never did anything to hurt her." She followed him into the living room and sat on the sofa, placing her purse on the coffee table.

He winced at the venom in her voice. "I don't know." Sure, he suspected Deb didn't like competing with an ex-wife and mother when she doubted her abilities as a second wife and stepmother, but he couldn't be certain. He tugged Adam toward the sofa, letting his son sit between him and his mother. "I guess she feels threatened by you."

"Me?" Stephanie widened her eyes, crossing one leg over the other. "She stole you, not the other way around."

"Yeah, well, she knows I have regrets." He twisted his mouth into a frown, remembering something from therapy. "I told her I've fallen out of love with her."

She dropped her arms into her lap and leaned closer. "You have?"

The surprise in her voice unsettled him. When he tucked an arm around his son's shoulders and held him close, he shifted on the sofa to avoid pinching the feeding tube. Warmth spread across his chest and down into his arms. What would his life look like if he had chosen to stay? Would Stephanie have managed his cancer diagnosis differently? All those speculative questions rose, begging to be answered. "Our counselor thinks my lack of love is caused by cancer. But I don't know. I think the problem is something else." He searched her face, hoping for an answer.

"Like what?" She placed an elbow on her knee and a chin in her hand.

"Like our divorce." He rubbed a hand along Adam's upper arm.

Adam squirmed and shimmied away. "Song."

"Go get your music, and I'll help you find a song." Cassidy waved toward the hallway.

Adam exited the room.

After uncrossing her legs, Stephanie scooted closer and frowned. "I don't understand."

Bowing his head, he scrubbed his face with both hands. "Sometimes I regret leaving."

Adam tottered into the room and flopped between

them, his elbows jutting out like wings. "Song." He jabbed his father in the ribs with the computer tablet.

"Careful." Cassidy winced, holding his side. He grabbed Adam's finger and showed him how to scroll up the screen. "Which one do you want?"

"Song." Adam tugged away his hand and the tablet and handed it to Stephanie.

Smiling, she swiped her finger across the screen and started his favorite song.

Adam tossed the computer tablet onto the coffee table. He sat on the sofa and squealed. Cupping his hands over his ears, he bounced up and down on the cushions. The sofa rippled, and he grinned. "Thank you." He gazed at his mother.

"You're welcome." Stephanie kissed his forehead and ruffled the hair on the back of his head.

Watching the tender exchange of mother and son, Cassidy ached. Why did he chastise Deb for the same behavior he found endearing between Stephanie and Adam? An embarrassing heat rushed to his face. If both women were so similar, then why did he walk away from one to be with the other? What had he hoped to gain? What had he lost? He bit his lower lip and wondered if he didn't fix his current relationship with Deb would he end up with no one.

Looking over Adam's head, Stephanie smiled. "I believe everything happens for a reason. If you hadn't left, I wouldn't have moved to LA and starred in a hit show. I finally have the career I've always wanted." She stood. "Do you need help making lunch?"

He gazed up into his ex-wife's luminous face, her smile wide and genuine, and her hand extended to help him up. Taking her soft fingers, he rose to his feet and followed her into the kitchen. Emotions lodged in his throat. He should be happy the family trinity was temporarily reunited, but he could only fret about what he had lost and what he might lose again.

****

Deb squinted through her sunglasses and tugged the cap over her forehead. The dry heat pelted through the sheer awning over the bleachers during the final game between the Florida Sunshine Seniors and the California Vine Valley Crushers for the title of World Masters Champions.

Hope nudged Deb's shoulder. "Ice chips?"

After scooping a handful out of the plastic cup, Deb dabbed the cold, marble-sized bits of ice on her cheeks and neck. As soon as the ice touched her skin, the hard bits melted, forming tiny rivers down her back that dried before they touched her hips. "What's the score?"

"Seventeen to twenty." Geraldine fanned her manicured nails in front of her face. "We need four runs to win."

Deb propped her elbows on her knees and cupped her chin in her hands.

The bases were loaded. The Sunshine pitcher walked Nick and Lionel, bringing runners across the plate for two runs.

Johnny strode up to bat.

Johnny was a great pitcher. Maybe even better than Cassidy. But he was a terrible batter. Maybe the worst on the team. He couldn't control his swing, always missing the sweet spot. Deb cringed, turning away. "I can't watch." She shuddered. "We really need Cassidy now."

Hope smiled, rubbing her shoulder. "Don't worry. Johnny can hit."

"As good as I can." Geraldine groaned.

"He's not *that* bad." Hope waved a hand toward the field, and her bracelets *clinked*. "He didn't strike out in all games."

Deb raised her fingers. "Only the last two."

The pitcher lobbed a high ball, and Johnny followed the arc with his gaze before swinging and missing.

The umpire shot up a fist. "Strike."

Tension snaked across Deb's jaw. "Doesn't look good, ladies."

The pitcher tossed another high ball.

Johnny hopped with a side step as he swung. The ball cracked against the sweet spot on the bat, and the low grounder traveled through the gap between second and third.

Geraldine stood, her hands cupped around her mouth. "Run!"

Johnny shot toward first, and two runners crossed home plate before the ball was thrown to second.

Hope grabbed Deb's hand and tugged her to her feet. "We won!"

A burst of adrenaline pumped through Deb's body. She released Hope's hand, tossed her cap into the air, and caught it. "Yippee!"

Geraldine folded the umbrella and tucked it into the cart along with the ice cooler. "Now the celebrations begin." She winked. "I'll meet you ladies in the dugout. I need to congratulate the captain of the team."

The team posed for a group photo and answered

questions from a local news reporter.

Deb lingered beside the cyclone fence, typing a text to Cassidy.

—We just won the World Masters. How are you doing?—

Glancing at the time on her phone, Deb speculated Cassidy was probably either resting in the recliner or waiting for the five o'clock news. A few seconds later, her phone chimed.

—I'm okay. What was the score? Who hit the winning run?—

Sighing, she considered how to phrase things, so Cassidy wouldn't take offense. He never liked Johnny, and he didn't need to know he was voted Most Valuable Player based on this evening's play. After a long moment, she typed.

—The score was twenty-one to twenty. We won by one run in the open.—

She tucked the phone in her back pocket and adjusted her cap.

The players received their trophy, T-shirts, and caps.

Lionel scooped her up for a hug and twirled her around. "Did you tell Cassidy we won?"

"Yes." She gasped. The firm and sweaty weight of his body contrasted sharply to the ridges of bone she felt when Cassidy hugged her. "I sent him a text."

"Tell him we'll drink a round of beers for him, too." Lionel set her on her feet and winked.

"No. I better not tell him, or he'll be jealous." She laughed, but pain hitched her voice. The phone chirped in her back pocket. After withdrawing it, she swiped the screen to read the message.

—Did Nick hit a homerun?—

Tension knotted her shoulders. Should she tell him the truth? Or just wait? Biting her lower lip, she typed.

—Nick was walked. So was Lionel. Johnny hit a double.—

Cupping the phone in her damp palm, she waited for another chime. When her phone buzzed again, she read the message.

—Should have been me.—

If the lineup hadn't changed and Cassidy had played instead of Johnny, then the statement would have been correct. Cassidy would have hit the winning run. He would be MVP, the team's hero.

—I'm sorry.—

The words seemed thin and futile so far away, but Deb didn't know what else to type. The phone beeped, warning of a low battery. She had forgotten to plug it into the charger last night. Lifting her head, she scanned the field and the dugout. Most of the players had left, wandering toward the concession stands, restrooms, or parking lot.

Out of the crowd, Hope emerged with Nick. "We're meeting at the restaurant next to the casino for dinner at seven. Do you need a ride back to the hotel?"

Nodding, Deb tucked the phone into her back pocket and hugged Nick to congratulate him on the win. In her arms, he felt tall and sturdy, everything she didn't feel right now. After all, her husband was over six hundred miles away, probably sitting on the recliner, doused in self-pity, while she was about to party hard with the winning team. How fair was that?

Chapter Twenty-Three

Moments after receiving the final text from Deb about the Vine Valley Crushers winning the World Masters, Cassidy sat on the recliner in the living room, cupping the phone in his hands.

Stephanie entered the room. "What's wrong?" Frowning, she sat on the sofa. "You look like you've received bad news."

Shaking his head, Cassidy forced a smile. "Good news, actually. The Vine Valley Crushers won the World Masters." He gripped the phone tighter. "John hit the winning run."

"Oh, I understand." Stephanie slapped her hands against her thighs and stood. "*You* should have hit the winning run, right?"

A faint heat bloomed against his skin. She knew him too well. Bowing his head, he leaned over and set the phone on the coffee table. "Yes. If I didn't have cancer—"

"But you do." She knelt, taking his hands in hers.

Her skin was as warm, soft, and comforting as he remembered. Tears welled up in his eyes, and he blinked back the storm of emotions in his chest. "I should have helped the team win."

She squeezed his hands. "Next year."

The fierce whisper matched the determined look in her eyes. How he missed her strength and persistence.

She never backed down from a challenge. Not even when the situation wasn't hers to fight.

"Don't worry about Johnny." She rubbed her fingers over his hands. "He was only subbing for you."

Adam wandered into the room, holding his computer tablet. "Song?"

After releasing Cassidy's hands, Stephanie rose and swiped her finger across the screen. She scrolled through the selection. "Here. Use *your* finger to make the music play." She tapped Adam's index finger against the icon, and a wail of guitars blasted from the speakers.

"Thank you." Adam snatched the computer tablet and darted out of the room.

Listening to his son squeal with delight, Cassidy smiled with old, familiar gratitude. "You're a great mom."

"And you're a great dad." She perched on the sofa beside him. "What about Deb? Isn't she a great stepmom?"

Shaking his head, Cassidy frowned. "She doesn't have patience. She doesn't tolerate half as much as you do." And, deep down, he wished she did. He also wished she understood him at the same level as Stephanie did.

"Give her time." Stephanie fiddled with her fingers, clasping and unclasping them. "She hasn't been with him since birth." After glancing at the clock on the wall, she gasped. "I should take Adam home and make dinner." Standing, she gathered her purse and keys.

"Why don't you stay?"

"For dinner?" She frowned, waving the keys. "We already stayed for lunch. We should go, so you can get some rest."

Panic rose in his raw throat. He didn't want to sit in a house full of loneliness. "When the house is quiet, I can't sleep."

She spun, snatching the remote off the bookcase. "Watch something." She clicked and flipped through the channels. "You can even watch me tonight. They're airing the last episode I filmed."

Why watch Stephanie play someone else on TV when he could talk with her in his living room? "No. I want you both to stay."

"Overnight?" She gaped, dropping the remote on the carpet. "I can't. I don't have my personal items."

He just lost the opportunity to win the World Masters. "I don't want to be alone." His voice was thick with emotion. The temptation to drink overshadowed her resistance. "Drive home and get them."

She bent and set the remote on the coffee table. Standing, she huffed. "I can't sleep in the bed you share with Deb."

"Sleep here." He pointed toward the sofa. "I don't mind."

Shaking her head, she swept her arm around the room. "Don't you know how hard it is to be in the same house I shared with you for over twenty years?" She dropped her arms to the sides and sniffled. "Everything is the same but different. Deb's special touches are everywhere." She jabbed a finger above the doorway. "Crucifixes in every room." She shuddered. "I feel like I'm in Sunday school again."

Cassidy studied the room from a fresh perspective. Before he only noticed the photographs, the new ones he had taken since Deb returned to his life, but now he glimpsed everything else—the Sacred Heart of Jesus on the wall beside the window, the statue of Mary beside the lamp on the end table, and the string of rosary beads in a glass dish on the coffee table. He also recognized what was missing. "Excuse me for a moment. I'll be right back." He stood and hobbled out of the room. In the hall closet, he tugged on a string and a set of stairs retracted from the attic. He stepped gingerly up the ladder into the dark, dusty space. After crawling on his knees, he found the box with the items he sought and dragged it back down the stairs. He set the box on the coffee table in the living room and wiped his hands on his pants. "These items are yours."

Stephanie removed the lid and lifted the first framed photograph in her hands. "Oh, my goodness. We look so young." She gasped, turning the frame toward him.

In the wedding picture, a pregnant, red-headed bride in a floor-length, white gown and a sandy-haired man in a tux with a red bow tie stood holding hands in this house's backyard. "We were so happy." Cassidy admired Stephanie's wistful smile in the photograph.

She giggled. "*I* was happy. You were drunk. See how red your skin was." She touched the image of what could have been a sunburned face.

Shame doused him. Back then, when wasn't he drinking? "Dr. Rodriguez thinks my cancer's from alcohol abuse." He dipped his head toward his chest.

"I'm not surprised." She lowered the photograph.

"But I'm in rehab." He picked up his pen and journal off the end table and flipped through the pages. "I feel like drinking right now. That's why I asked you to stay. Most of the time, I just write instead. Dr. Chang calls my notebook the cancer diaries."

She set aside the photograph and extended a hand. "May I read one?"

No one read any of these entries outside of therapy. Not even Deb. Cassidy clutched the pages to his chest for a moment before glimpsing the genuine glimmer of curiosity in Stephanie's eyes. "They're just rough drafts." He swallowed and winced against the tightness in his throat. Over the weeks, the words flowed from random thoughts into coherent poems. Tough and brittle little poems like the feelings in his heart.

"I've always liked your writing, especially your poems." Taking the book in her hands, she scanned the words. The smile dissolved on her lips, and a faint color rose in her cheeks. Lowering the journal, she widened her eyes. "Cass, these poems..." Shaking her head, she clenched a fist to her chest. "Does Deb know you feel this way?"

Shame blanketed his shoulders. Deb didn't know. No one knew, except Stephanie. He sighed and retrieved the journal.

"You need to tell her." Stephanie touched his palm. "Or I will."

Bowing his head, Cassidy reread the words.

I'm tired of my nauseous,
weak,
dehydrated,
done
body.
I don't want to die
withered,
falling,
bare,

alone.

"I don't always feel this way." He closed the book and searched her face. "Sometimes I'm happy."

She stepped closer and placed a hand on his forearm. "How do you feel now?"

Her fingers burned through his skin and settled onto his bones. The touch anchored him to this moment. The old love he felt for her rushed forward, and the new love he felt for Deb rushed back until the two emotions swam on top of each other, causing him to feel like he might drown. "I'm overwhelmed." He sniffed once before the tears slipped down his cheeks. "I thought I had everything all figured out, but I don't." Shaking his head, he sank onto the sofa. "I'm sorry for walking out on our marriage. I wasn't thinking clearly. I just needed to escape, and I took the first road out." He snuffled, wiping the tears from his eyes with the back of his hand. "Sometimes I just want this life to be over." He hitched a breath, his voice trembling. "The pain is too much."

Frowning, she grabbed his hands. "Fight, Cass. You've got to fight. We love you too much."

The pinched expression in her face matched the pain in his chest. "How can you love me after I left you and broke up our family?"

Smiling, she gripped his hands tighter. "I forgave you years ago. Time you forgive yourself."

Through the blur of tears, he gazed at her hands on top of his, the long fingers and tapered nails. How could she forgive him for hurting her?

"Listen." She rubbed a thumb along his knuckles. "I'm not giving up, so you can't give up, either."

He nodded, holding her gaze. "But I messed up."

"We all mess up—just part of being human." She squeezed his hands before letting go. Standing, she slapped her thighs and smiled. "Why don't we go for a ride? We can stop by my place, so I can get my overnight bag. We'll come back here, and I'll make dinner. Adam and I will spend the night." She waved a hand toward the TV. "Who knows? Maybe we can watch how ridiculous I look in a gray wig playing the matriarch of a big, crazy family." She tilted her head and widened her smile. "What do you say?"

Thinking, he blinked. What could he say? She was here, in his living room, agreeing to spend the night near him. He would not be alone. "Sure." He stood on wobbly knees. "Get Adam." A deep feeling of satisfaction and relief tingled in his arms and legs. "Let's go." Tonight he would be with his old family. Why worry about the day after tomorrow when Deb would return home?

****

After a quick breakfast of tangy orange juice and burnt toast from room service, Deb slipped into a pink, satin, tea-length dress and wove a strand of baby's breath through her hair. She removed Lionel's wedding band from the red velvet box and slipped it over her thumb for safekeeping. After taking a crowded elevator to the lobby, she strolled through the loud casino past the conference rooms to the chapel. Her heels sunk into the plush red carpet, and the serene quiet enveloped her like an embrace. The doors were open, and Hope and Nick stood side by side before the row of pews leading up to the altar.

The chapel was breathtaking in a rich blend of earth tones, dark woods, modern artwork, and glass-beaded lights. A pianist sat behind a baby grand, playing tinkling music. The air-conditioning hummed overhead, chilling the room to the perfect temperature. The elegant altar, draped in white linens, occupied the center of the room. A faint whiff of roses lingered in the air.

"Good morning, you two." Deb smiled, drinking in the sight of Hope's shimmery, pink, floor-length gown and Nick's black tux and purple bow tie.

A hotel wedding coordinator carried a basket full of sweet-smelling gardenias. "Here are your bouquets, ladies."

A tremor of anticipation zinged through her body, and Deb dipped her head to breathe in the refreshing scent. "Where is everybody?"

Nick chuckled. "Most of the team flew home this morning. We're the only ones who stayed."

"Really?" Deb lifted her head and widened her eyes. "All this fuss for the three of us?"

"Four."

With a glance over her shoulder, Deb glimpsed John standing beneath the threshold in a black tux. A flash of anger sizzled in her belly. "Are you subbing for Cassidy?"

Shaking his head, John laughed. "I can't replace your husband." He clasped his hands in front of his thighs and smiled. "I'm here because Lionel asked. I don't have anywhere else to be."

Hope matched his smile. "Enjoying retirement?"

"More than I did coaching high school baseball or teaching math." He flashed his wide smile, and his glimmering eyes twinkled above his freckled cheeks.

Nick playfully jabbed his side. "I don't blame

you."

He resembled his sister, Stephanie. Deb clenched the bouquet in her tight fist, a jolt of anger spiking her blood. Why did he have to be here to remind her of her husband's absence?

The hotel wedding coordinator returned. "Let's move everyone to the altar." She waved her hands from side to side. "Women on the left, men on the right."

When Deb imagined the renewal of wedding vows in Las Vegas, she envisioned a cheap five-and-dime, drive-through chapel with Elvis as the officiant, and not a glamorous, first-class chapel in one of the larger, more modern hotels on the strip. Standing by the classy, tasteful altar, clutching a fresh bouquet, she felt a rush of expectation. She remembered her own wedding in Saint Peter's Church with Father Anthony presiding, the air thick and redolent with the scent of incense, and Geraldine and Lionel served as the matron of honor and best man, respectively. Now the roles were reversed, and Deb couldn't help but think of Cassidy, wondering how he was doing alone.

Maybe I shouldn't have come. Guilt snaked up her back. *Maybe I should have flown home last night after the team won.*

When she sent a text this morning, she received a message from Cassidy that he was fine. She bit her lower lip. Was he telling the truth? Since his diagnosis, nothing had been fine with either of them, separately or together. But they had been attending couples' counseling and practicing new communication skills. She released her lip and straightened her spine. Surely, she could trust him.

A few loud chords jolted her attention to the open

double doors.

Lionel stepped beneath the threshold dressed in a black tux and purple bow tie, with a single, white gardenia pinned to the lapel of his jacket. The white, flowing mane streamed across his shoulders like a mantle. Smiling, he marched down the aisle in pace with the music.

The chords brightened, and the processional song began.

Geraldine swept into the room in a slinky, white, floor-length gown with a train beaded in sequins and pearls. A diamond tiara and a veil that brushed against her shoulders adorned her golden halo of hair. Her long fingers clutched a bouquet of white roses, gardenias, and baby's breath. She floated down the aisle, a wide grin creasing her face.

How radiant. Deb gasped.

A photographer trailed her, snapping pictures.

At the altar, Geraldine handed Deb her bouquet and grabbed Lionel's outstretched hands.

The officiant bowed his head and read from a prepared speech. "Geraldine and Lionel, today we celebrate a renewal of your commitment to love, honor, and cherish each other. Most people believe marriage is the final step in a love relationship. But you both know the challenges marriage brings, from the hurts that require forgiveness, to the disappointments that require understanding, and to the effort of turning toward each other when it is so much easier to turn away. This ceremony is to celebrate the victory of your commitment to continue to love under all circumstances."

Listening, Deb dipped her head to her chest. A pain

hardened in her solar plexus. She flattened a palm against her ribs, breathing into the knot. Her thoughts spiraled out of control. Cassidy no longer loved her. She couldn't inspire that spark again, no matter how many couples' therapy sessions she attended.

"When I was sixteen, you came over to the store and asked my father if you could take me out to dinner." Geraldine repeated the vows she wrote. "He gave you twenty dollars and a six-pack of beer and told you to have me home by eleven. We ate at Lulu's Pizza and drank the beer in your pickup truck. You had me home by ten. My father said, 'Why don't you keep her?' And I thought, 'Yeah, sugar. Why don't you?' And you did."

Deb bristled, pushing back her shoulders. *Why am I here watching someone else's love story? I should be home making my own.*

As he gripped Geraldine's hands, Lionel chuckled. "I didn't keep you that night, but I held you in my heart from the moment I laid eyes on you." Shaking his head, he smiled. "I couldn't get you out of my mind with your blonde hair, long legs, and girlish giggle. I nicknamed you Golden Goddess right after our first kiss. Over the years, I've shorted it to GG, but you're my Golden Goddess just the same."

No one could hear Deb's soundless foot tapping, but the anxiety ratcheting in her blood pounded like drums in her ears. Could she skip the reception, take a cab to the airport, and book the next flight home? Every second away from Cassidy was one less second together. How many moments was she wasting being here with her friends?

"You may exchange rings." The officiant nodded.

Lost in thought, Deb didn't respond until Hope nudged her ribs. With a brief yelp, she withdrew the ring from her warm thumb and handed it to Geraldine—a solid gold band inscribed with today's date and the couple's initials inside. Just like the new dress, Geraldine wanted new rings to symbolize beginning a new chapter of their lives together.

"With this ring, I renew our love." Geraldine slipped the band onto Lionel's finger.

He repeated the gesture with a similar gold band.

The officiant waved a hand between the couple. "It is with great pleasure that I conclude this renewal of your marriage vows. You may celebrate with a kiss."

Lionel tucked the veil behind the tiara and cupped his wife's face with his broad hands. With puckered lips, he kissed her mouth.

"You call that peck a kiss?" Geraldine threw her arms around his neck, holding him close. "Let me show you a kiss." She tilted her head and nudged his lips apart with her tongue.

He dropped his hands to her hips and tugged her closer.

Cheers and clapping erupted from the bridal party.

Hope sniffled, dabbing the corners of her eyes with a handkerchief.

Only Deb glanced at the exit. *I need to leave.* The levity in the air suffocated her. At her earliest opportunity, she thrust the bridal bouquet into Geraldine's arms and hugged her goodbye. "Congratulations. I can't stay for the reception. I need to go home."

Geraldine wiggled out of the embrace and frowned. "Sugar, is everything okay with Cassidy?"

Deb nodded. "I just need to be with him. I don't know how much time we have left."

"Go." Geraldine ushered her down the aisle. "Give him our best."

Without a word, Deb rushed out of the chapel and through the chaotic casino. Smoke twirled around her, making her stomach queasy. When she arrived at the bank of elevators, she jabbed the glowing, white button several times. *Hurry, hurry, hurry.* Tapping a foot, she wondered if her marriage was over or if she would be granted a second chance.

Chapter Twenty-Four

Cassidy wanted Stephanie and Adam to stay one more night.

"I can't." Stephanie slung her purse over her shoulder and grabbed her overnight bag from the sofa. Evening sunlight flooded the living room. "I promised Johnny I'd pick him up from the airport tomorrow morning. Adam and I need to get home, so I can make dinner and get Adam to sleep at a decent time." She nudged Adam toward the foyer. "Say goodbye to Dad."

"Bye." Adam flapped a hand.

"Not yet, buddy." Cassidy slipped on a pair of shoes. "I'll walk you to the truck." He followed them out the front door. A cool, balmy breeze rustled through the browning leaves on the apple tree. The sky was still blue. Cassidy held open the door of the black pickup truck and waited for Adam to fasten the seatbelt. He was thankful for this time with his old family, from listening to Stephanie sing goodnight songs to Adam to talking with Stephanie deep into the night. Remembering the box of photographs on the coffee table, Cassidy slapped his forehead. "I'll be right back. I forgot the pictures." He hobbled inside the house, hoisted the box into his arms, and dashed outside.

A car door slammed, and a ride-sharing vehicle sped off. Deb stood on the sidewalk with luggage beside her. She pointed toward Stephanie. "Cass, what's *she* doing here?"

Her sharp voice stabbed him. Hugging the box against his thundering heartbeat, he gulped. Dread crashed over him. He breathed hard through his nose. Why did he always have to choose between his old life and his new life?

Grimacing, Stephanie took a step forward. "We were just leaving." She narrowed her gaze and dumped her overnight bag on the passenger's seat. "I came to pick up some photos Cassidy neglected to give me after our divorce."

After a stuttering glance from Deb to Stephanie, Cassidy nudged the box next to the overnight bag.

Stephanie shut the door and strode around the truck. "Say goodbye to your father."

"Bye, Dad." Adam flapped his hand.

A moment of tenderness powered through Cassidy. He bent and kissed his son's forehead. "Be good for your mom, buddy." He ruffled his hair and smiled. "Bye." After he shut the door, he nodded toward Stephanie. He wanted to open his arms and encircle her body, pressing her close and squeezing out all the sadness. Only his fear of the distrustful, angry look blazing in Deb's eyes stopped him. Instead, he gave a pathetic wave. "Thanks for stopping by." He only hoped the love he felt transferred to his gaze.

Stephanie's lips tilted up. "You're welcome. Thanks for the photos." She climbed inside the cab and started the engine.

As soon as the pickup truck turned the corner, Cassidy sighed. The distressed tension slackened from his shoulders. Turning, he grabbed the handle of Deb's luggage and strolled inside the house.

Her footsteps shuffled behind him. "Why didn't you tell me she was coming over?"

The accusatory tone of her voice raked against his nerves. Stopping, he spun and narrowed his gaze. "Why didn't you tell me you were coming home a day early?"

Throwing open her arms, she widened her eyes. "I wanted to surprise you."

What a terrible surprise. Heaving a sigh, he deposited her luggage in the untouched bedroom and returned to the messy living room. He wanted a moment alone. But Deb trailed him like a shadow. Her hostile glare scanned the room before resting on something behind him. He spun, fully expecting to see his ex-wife through the window. No one was outside—just the apple tree with the wind whistling through its leaves. He faced Deb again. She was still staring over his shoulder, her expression stony and trancelike.

She pointed. "Why is a blanket on the sofa?"

He followed her gaze. Sure enough, the blanket Stephanie curled beneath last night dangled like a disembodied arm from the cushions. He swallowed, remembering how they sat side by side watching her over-the-top performance as a gray-haired matriarch of a big, unwieldy family on the night-time drama. He remembered how the laughter buoyed him, giving him hope. Deb's anger drained him. He shrugged. "I was cold."

She stepped around him and snatched the blanket, bringing it to her nose. "Why does it smell like *her*?" She shook the material at his face.

The scent of vanilla and lavender ignited sweet memories of snuggling with Stephanie, watching TV, their heads tipped against each other. He had forgotten those happy days of his first marriage.

"Did she spend the night?"

A frantic, wild-eyed hatred danced in her eyes, and her skin flushed red. All of his defenses crumpled. He spread his arms wide. "I was lonely. I wanted to see Adam."

"How could you?" she screamed, spittle flying from her open mouth. "How could you?" She raised her arm, brandishing the blanket like a sword.

Afraid she might strike, he ducked.

She took a step back and lowered her arm, dropping the blanket and her shoulders. "Why can't you love me anymore?"

The brokenness in her voice troubled him. He took two steps forward, touching her stiff shoulders. In spite of the angry tango, an ember of that innocent love glowed in the fire of hostility and fear. He wrapped his arms around her, pulling her to his chest. "I *do* love you." He kissed her forehead and caressed the length of her arms with his warm hands.

"What about Stephanie?" She wrestled out of his embrace and stared into his eyes.

He swallowed. How could he tell her the truth without hurting her? He grasped her hands. "We're on friendly terms."

"Friendly terms?" She stepped back, tugging her hands free. "Do you mean you *like* her?"

He bowed his head and knotted his hands. "I don't *hate* her anymore."

"How can you love her *and* me?"

Raising his head, he pointed toward the crucifix above the doorway. "The same way you can love Him *and* me."

Gaping, she swiveled her gaze from him to the doorway and back again. "That love is different."

Frowning, he broadened his stance. "I'm not apologizing for being friends with Stephanie."

She gaped. "So, now you're *friends*?"

He shrugged. "Why not? She's the mother of my son. She didn't do anything wrong. I did." He blinked, feeling tightness spread across his ribs. "I broke up my family."

Huffing, she curled her arms across her chest. "I don't want you to be friends with your ex-wife."

He pointed toward the crucifix. "Didn't Jesus command us to love our neighbors like ourselves?" He sighed. "Stephanie is our neighbor."

Throwing up her arms, she widened her eyes. "I can't believe I'm getting religion lessons from my husband who doesn't believe in anything greater than himself." She swiveled, grabbed her purse, and stamped out of the room. "I never should have left God."

With tight fists, he followed her into the foyer. "You can always go back."

She jangled her keys, shaking her head. "Maybe I will." A gust of chilled air swept into the room. She exited the house, slamming the front door.

The pictures on the walls rattled. Heaving a sigh, he rubbed the goose bumps on his arms. The roar of a car's engine rumbled away into silence. He hated being alone. The emptiness of the room ticked like a time bomb in his ears. He scratched the stubble on his rough chin. Loneliness gaped all around him. Why had he driven his wife away?

****

As Deb entered the dark church, she felt the quiet

settle against her shoulders, calming the inner turmoil swirling inside her chest. With hands clutched in prayer, she padded down the aisle. A musky smell filled the air. At the altar, she genuflected before ducking into an alcove and lighting a candle beneath a statue of Saint Monica, the patron saint of troubled marriages. The flickering light cast shadows across the worn and wrinkled face of the saint whose troubles mirrored her own. A pang of grief and worry clutched her chest. How could anyone endure years of torture being married to a pagan? She knelt and bowed her head, praying for the saint to intercede on her behalf. She needed someone to plead her case with God and inspire Cassidy to see the error of his ways.

"Good evening, Deb."

She lifted her head and glimpsed Father Anthony. He was dressed in a full collar shirt and black cassock.

"I'm closing the church." Smiling, he bowed closer and touched his watch. "I'll give you five more minutes, okay?"

Tension tightened across her jaw, and she nodded. Hoping for some peace from her problems, she bowed her head and prayed.

The bench creaked and shifted with extra weight. He knelt beside her.

The warmth of his nearness awakened her senses. He smelled strong and musky like a hard day at work. She opened her eyes, remembering the first time she glimpsed Cassidy after thirty years. He stood in her mother's kitchen, sweaty from repairing the broken air-conditioner. He smelled just like Father Anthony, honest and hardworking. A tremor shot through her. He was also married to the woman she now hated, the woman he wanted to be friends with, and the same woman who drove her to her knees in an otherwise-empty church on a weekday night. Distracted, she swept her fingers over her forehead, chest, and across her shoulders. She stood, blew out the candle, and strolled down the aisle.

Father Anthony hustled after her. "You didn't have to leave so soon." The keys clattered in his hands against the double doors.

"I couldn't focus once you knelt beside me." A bristle of irritation rubbed beneath her skin. She bit her lower lip to stop the pain.

"I'll walk you to your car." He gestured toward the parking lot.

Shaking her head, she wrapped her arms tight across her waist. A brisk chill settled against her shoulders. She shuddered. Why had she neglected to bring a sweater? "I don't want to leave."

He cocked his head to the side. "What's the trouble?"

She glanced at the intense darkness of the sky. With Nick and Hope in Las Vegas for one more night and Lionel and Geraldine off to Europe for their second honeymoon, Father Anthony was the closest thing she had to a friend. She leveled her gaze. "My husband wants to be friends with his ex-wife." The statement sounded so matter-of-fact. Why did the words cut like a knife?

Pursing his lips, he nodded. "And you don't want him to, am I correct?"

"I wish she would disappear from our lives." She waved a hand like a magic wand. "I know she can't because she's the mother of my stepson, but I wish she would." She slumped her shoulders. "Am I a bad person for thinking this way, Father?"

"Not hardly." He chuckled, thrusting his hands into his pockets. "Saint Joseph was Jesus' stepfather. I'm sure he was frustrated with God several times."

She gasped, clasping a hand over her mouth. *He's right.* When Joseph found out Mary was pregnant with God's child, Joseph wanted to leave her. An angel spoke in his dream, convincing him to stay. God wanted Joseph to marry the pregnant virgin and raise Jesus as his own. Joseph could have left. But he didn't. He stayed. He cared for Jesus, just as she cared for Adam. Hot shame burned her skin. "I was praying to the wrong saint."

"No saint is the wrong saint. They all intercede for us." He motioned toward the parking lot. "Go home. Make up with your husband. Just like Saint Joseph did with Mary."

But I'm not a saint. She swallowed the tightness in her throat. *I'm not ready to go home.* She flashed a wan smile. "Thank you for your counsel, Father. Good night." Pivoting, she strolled down the steps and across the pavement to her car. After starting the engine, she drove downtown to Courthouse Square. The streets were lit with fairytale lights strung on the trees' branches. Couples strolled arm in arm along the sidewalk.

A few turns away, she noticed the neon lights signaling Jasper's Bar and Grill. The establishment was open until midnight. With her heartbeat thudding in her chest, she steered into a parking spot. She hustled across the sidewalk, bristling against the bitter cold, and stepped into the restaurant's warm, enveloping glow and friendly chatter.

From the bar, Elliot waved. "Hello, sister."

She smiled, suddenly thankful for a familiar face. Taking a seat at the bar, she hung her purse on a hook beneath the counter and ordered a glass of the house red wine.

"What brings you here?" Elliot set the glass on a coaster and leaned against the counter with a dish rag in his hands.

His green eyes glittered like the lights over the bar. He seemed genuinely interested in her and her problems. Over the months, she resisted his friendship, wary of his intentions. After taking a sip of the sweet, acidic fluid, she forced a smile. "Marriage problems." Glancing down, she twirled the stem of the glass between her fingers. The ruby fluid swirled around and around, releasing an aromatic scent of oak and berries. "Apparently, Father Anthony thinks I should be gracious and let my husband be friends with his ex-wife."

Elliot tossed back his head and scoffed. "Father Anthony has never been married. He doesn't know what he's talking about." He slapped the counter with the rag and shook his head. "When my wife was ill, I was lucky. No exes came back to haunt us. But I was a scoundrel just the same, looking for comfort outside the home."

Knowing his history with Geraldine, she assumed the worst. "You cheated?"

He tipped his head to the side. "I was tired, lonely, and scared to lose the love of my life." He shrugged. "What else was I to do?"

She sighed, shaking her head. "I don't have that

problem."

"Yes, you do." He held her gaze. "You don't trust him around his ex, which says a lot."

"Fidelity isn't the issue." She took another sip and felt the warmth travel to her belly and float along her legs. "He can't have sex right now. He's toxic."

Wrinkling his forehead, he frowned. "I'm not talking about sex. I'm talking about intimacy."

The sudden change in the tone of his voice jostled her, and she sat straighter. "What are you saying?"

He crossed his arms on the counter. "I'm saying you need to go home and talk. Tell him all the things you're telling me. Then be quiet and listen."

Listen? Heat invaded her cheeks. Did he contact Stephanie because he needed someone to just listen? Fresh shame scalded her, and she doused the flames with another gulp of bittersweet wine. "Oh, how could I have got things so wrong?" Rummaging in her purse, she tossed a twenty-dollar bill on the counter and grabbed her purse. "Thank you for the wine and the advice." She paused, fiddling with the straps of the purse. A realization crept over her, and she shivered with the truth. "You and I are friends."

He shrugged. "We're members of the same faith—more of a spiritual family than neighborhood friends."

Deb heaved a sigh, knowing what she would tell Father Anthony the next time she was in the confessional: *My husband wants to heal his broken family. I am sorry I prevented him from being friends with his ex-wife.* She steeled her shoulders. "Good night, Elliot."

"Good luck, sister." He waved.

After stepping into the brisk night, she slipped into

the chilly car and started the engine. Glancing at the clock on the dash, she read the time. Eleven-thirty. She closed her eyes briefly and said a short prayer. *Jesus, Mary, Joseph, pray for us*. After shifting into Reverse, she backed out of the parking spot. *The holy family was a stepfamily. Just like my family*. She threw the gear into Drive and rammed her foot against the accelerator, determined to make things right.

Chapter Twenty-Five

Eleven forty-five. Cassidy glanced at the clock above the fireplace and kept pacing, wearing a pattern in the carpet with his feet. Panting, he bent and rubbed his tired legs with both hands. With their friends all out of town and the church closed, he didn't know where Deb could be. She wasn't a big drinker or a gambler, so the bars and casino were out of the question. Churning gnawed his stomach. Where was she?

The unbearable silence threw his thoughts into a tailspin. He grabbed his phone from his back pocket and texted Stephanie.

—*Deb left hours ago. What can I do to get her to come home?*—

A few moments passed before his phone chimed. Pausing on his endless pace, he swiped a finger across the screen.

—*Do nothing. Let her calm down. She'll be back. Be patient. XOXO.*—

Reading over the hugs and kisses once more, he smiled. Warmth radiated from his chest and into his arms and legs. At least, he managed to repair a relationship with one woman. He hoped Stephanie was right. Closing his eyes, he squeezed the phone against his heart. He couldn't bear the thought of losing Deb.

A car's engine rumbled into the cul-de-sac. He opened his eyes. Headlights swung across the curtains of the living room window. Anticipation lurched into his throat. After tucking the phone into his back pocket, he strode into the foyer and threw open the front door. A gust of chilled air blew into the room, pocking his skin with goose bumps. He shivered, watching Deb stroll up the driveway, a determined look on her fierce face.

She barreled into the room and clicked the door shut. After dropping her purse on the tile entryway, she flung her arms around his back and buried her cold face against his chest. "I'm sorry for storming off. I was angry." She clutched the material of his T-shirt in tight fists. When she lifted her face, she quivered. "I went to church to pray, and Father Anthony sent me away."

Frowning, he stroked the softness of her short hair with his fingers. "Where have you been?" He couldn't imagine her driving aimlessly around town, circling the city with her thoughts.

She gulped. "At Jasper's. Talking with Elliot." She hiccupped, placing her fingers over her lips. "I had a glass of wine."

The impulse to shove her away, dart out the door, and drive to the nearest liquor store shot through him like a flash of light. He ground his teeth. Blood rushed to his face. Why could she indulge when he couldn't? Taking a deep breath, he focused on his feelings, instead of needing to escape. "Why were you drinking at Jasper's? You said you'd never go back to that place after what happened between Elliot and Geraldine."

She uncurled her hands and placed her palms flat against his chest. "I didn't want to come home. I didn't want to fight about Stephanie."

Something else was going on. "If you wanted a

drink, you could have gone to the casino. Why did you choose Jasper's?"

She sighed. "I needed to talk to a friend."

"A friend?" He laughed, shaking his head. "What a hypocrite you are. You won't let me be friends with my ex-wife, but you're allowed to be friends with the man who almost ended your best friend's marriage."

Gaping, she dropped her hands from his chest and took a step back. "You're right." Glancing away, she shook her head. "I mean, I didn't plan on being friends with Elliot. He kept showing up while I was at church, being concerned about your welfare. I guess, over time, I viewed him in a different light."

"Stephanie isn't a threat. I won't leave you." He took a step closer, grasping for her cold hands. "If you are friends with Elliot, may I please be friends with my ex-wife?"

"How can you be friends when she's still in love?" She lifted her chin.

He sighed, squeezing her hands. How could he reassure her? "I know she loves me." He swallowed the tightness in his throat. "But *I* am in love with you."

"You *are*?" She gasped and widened her eyes.

"Yes, of course, I am. I always have been. I just didn't feel it." He released her hands and wrapped an arm around her shoulders. Steering, he guided her to the living room. With one swift motion, he grabbed his journal from the coffee table and placed it in her hands. "Since I stopped drinking, I've been writing about my feelings." He didn't tell her about sharing his poems with Stephanie first. He trusted his ex-wife wouldn't confide that bit of information to Deb. For a second, he held his breath to calm a twinge of nervousness. "I want you to know what's been going on inside of me since the diagnosis."

She clutched the journal and sat on the sofa. Opening the pages, she bowed her head and read.

He perched beside her, hands clasped in his lap to calm his twitchy muscles.

Mouthing the words, she flipped the page. Lifting her head, she widened her eyes and gasped. "Why didn't you tell me your depression was that bad?"

He shrugged, twisting his sweaty hands. "I couldn't. I didn't know how." He bowed his head, pressing his leg against her thigh. "I felt trapped. Whenever we talked, we ended up fighting. You always nagged. I always battled back. We never communicated." He sighed, releasing his hands and spreading his fingers wide. "All that conflict made me believe I had fallen out of love."

She dipped her head and read some more. Softness rounded her shoulders. Raising her head, she pointed. "You wrote this one for me?"

Her eyes shone. A warm sensation filled him, and he smiled. "Yes. I wrote a lot of those poems for you. I just never shared them until now. I didn't feel safe when we were fighting."

"I don't want to fight anymore." Shaking her head, she set aside the journal. With her fingertips, she stroked the side of his face. "I want to make up however best we can."

He turned his head, kissing her fingertips. He wanted to scoop her into his arms, carry her to the bedroom, toss her on the mattress, and cover her with kisses, but he couldn't. Brushing his lips against her fingers, he hummed. "When I get better, I'll show you how much I love you."

She giggled, tracing his lips with her fingers. "Oh, I bet you will."

After wrapping his arms around her, he drew her close. With their bodies squeezed together, he listened to their joint heartbeats stumble after one another. He closed his eyes and kissed her neck—once, twice, and three times.

She shivered.

He tugged at the hem of her shirt, slipping his fingers against her cool skin, warming her with his touch.

She closed her eyes and moaned. "We can't."

"Just let me hold you." He slipped his hands from underneath her shirt and placed them firmly against her back.

She circled her arms around him, melting her body against his. "I love you."

Closing his eyes, he kissed her forehead. "I love you more." He tightened his hold, feeling all of the tension drain from their relationship, leaving only peace.

Epilogue
Thanksgiving

Deb circled the long, mahogany dining room table beneath the crystal chandelier in Nick and Hope's mansion on Wapi Mountain. She placed the silverware wrapped in linen napkins next to each place setting. The warm smells of roasted turkey and gravy wafted into the room from the kitchen. "Thanks for hosting dinner this year."

"Of course." Hope nodded, filling each goblet with sparkling water from a pitcher. "Nick and I wanted to celebrate the good news."

Good news, indeed. Just thinking about Cassidy's last PET scan filled her with gratitude. The cancer was gone, not a trace left in his body, and the feeding tube had been removed. Over the past several weeks, he gained some weight and returned to work, after the successful grand reopening of Larry's Deli.

The door swung open, and a rush of guests flowed into the room.

Geraldine carried a carved turkey on a silver platter. "I hope you're hungry." She adjusted the turkey on the table beneath the twinkling lights. "Lionel brought too much food."

"I did not." Lionel set a bowl of mashed potatoes and a boat of gravy beside the turkey. "We're feeding nine people."

Nick placed bowls of green salad at each end of the table. "We can always send everyone home with leftovers."

"Or feed the homeless." John winked, taking a seat.

Stephanie led Adam by the hand. "Want to sit next to Uncle John?"

"Dad." Adam plopped into a chair and glanced over his shoulder.

Cassidy shuffled into the room and kissed Deb. "Thanks for letting Stephanie and John come," he whispered into her ear.

She nodded, hugging him tighter. The suggestion to invite them both hadn't been a knee-jerk reaction, but a deliberate attempt to set aside history for the sake of family and friendship.

After taking a seat next to his son, Cassidy patted the vacant chair beside him.

Deb smiled, joining him at the table. She curled her fingers around his warm hand.

Nick stood at the head of the table and tapped a fork against the rim of his glass. "Let's have a toast to the man of honor, Cassidy." He nodded toward his friend. "Congratulations on a clean bill of health. May you continue to regain your weight and your strength, so you can return to pitching for the Vine Valley Crushers next season."

"Hear, hear." Deb lifted her glass and *clinked* the rim against the others' glasses across the dining room table. She took a sip of the cold, sparkling water.

Cassidy waved his glass. "I want to thank my family and friends for supporting me on this journey. I couldn't have made it through without all of your help." He glanced at his wife and nodded. "And a special thanks to Deb, for being the best wife ever."

Heat crept across her cheeks. She dipped her chin to her chest, smiling.

"Ah, sugar. Let's eat." Geraldine swept her gaze across the table. "Something's missing." She tapped her chin with a finger, then widened her eyes. "Cranberry sauce. Be right back."

Deb loaded her plate with turkey, gravy, mashed potatoes, and green salad, passing on the cranberry sauce. Taking a bite of the warm, buttery potatoes, she glanced around the table. A soft feeling of contentment spread throughout her chest.

Lionel cut a piece of turkey and dipped it into some gravy. "Are you looking forward to getting back to acting?"

As she chewed, Stephanie nodded. "I've mixed feelings only because I'll miss all of you." She widened her smile. "But I'll be back during spring break to take care of Adam, so Cassidy and Deb can finally take that honeymoon in Hawaii."

"Oh, sugar. You have to take pictures for us." Geraldine clapped her hands.

Deb groaned, remembering how Geraldine subjected her and Hope to an hour slide show of all the sights she and Lionel experienced in London and Paris during their second honeymoon in Europe. "I'm not taking a bunch of pictures. I'll be too busy enjoying the experience." She motioned toward Cassidy. "Besides, you can read about the whole trip after Cassidy publishes his second book of poems."

Cassidy lifted his eyebrows. "What second book?"

"The one you'll write in the mornings while I'm lying in bed sleeping until noon." Deb winked, thankful for the release of tension and the return of playfulness.

Cassidy chuckled, wrapping an arm around the back of her chair. "What makes you think I'll let you sleep till noon?"

Another wave of heat crashed against her skin, and she kissed his cheek. "You always wake up early to write. When you're on vacation, why change your routine?"

"She's right." Cassidy shook his head. "She knows me too well."

Hope smiled. "What will your second book be about?"

Cassidy shrugged. "How should I know? I haven't written it yet."

"What about the cancer poems?" Stephanie asked.

A sharp twinge of pain shot across Deb's chest. Frowning, she glanced across the table at Stephanie's curious gaze then turned toward Cassidy. The blank expression on his face told her nothing. "How do you know about the cancer poems?"

Stephanie widened her eyes and touched her fingers to her collarbone. "Well, I—just assumed— Cassidy was writing about that experience."

A prickle of awareness traveled across Deb's scalp. *He shared the poems with her.* She stroked the napkin in her lap. *Relax. He also shared them with me.*

Cassidy lowered his fingers to Deb's hand. "Everyone knows I write about everything."

The tenderness of his gentle squeeze reassured her. Smiling, she gripped her husband's hand tighter, knowing she also held his heart. With God's help, she and Cassidy would continue to grow closer, keeping their never-ending promises to each other.

A word about the author…

Angela Lam is the author of several novels, a short story collection, and a memoir. The Women of the Crush series features a group of girlfriends exploring the challenges of their lives with their senior softball tournament team men in the imaginary Northern California town of Vine Valley.

Other Titles by This Author
Friends First
Love Again, Women of the Crush book 1
Now and Forever, Women of the Crush book 2
The Divorce Planner